PRAISE FOR LAIRD BARRON'S
ISAIAH COLERIDGE SERIES

"Isaiah Coleridge [is] an intimidating presence...A big bruiser who likes nothing better than a good fight."
—*The New York Times Book Review*

"Like a lyricist, Laird Barron excels at manipulating the tones and cadence of language."
—*Associated Press*

"Massive, scarred Isaiah is a thug's thug, but he's also a well-read student of mythology. He's indifferent to stab wounds and generates righteous mayhem in his quest. Fans of violent crime fiction will love this one and will be eager to hear more from Isaiah."
—*Booklist (starred review)*

ALSO BY LAIRD BARRON

NOVELS
The Croning
The Light is the Darkness

THE ISAIAH COLERIDGE SERIES
Blood Standard
Black Mountain
Worse Angels

NOVELLAS
Man With No Name
X's for Eyes

COLLECTIONS
The Imago Sequence and Other Stories
Occultation and Other Stories
The Beautiful Thing That Awaits Us All (Stories)
Swift to Chase (Stories)

THE WIND BEGAN TO HOWL

LAIRD BARRON

The Wind Began to Howl
Copyright © 2023 by Laird Barron
Print ISBN: 979-8988128601

Front Cover Art & Design by Mayra Fersner | HagCult.com
Book Spread & Design by Todd Keisling | Dullington Design Co.
Author Photo by Jessica M.

No part of this work may be reproduced or transmitted in any form or by any means without permission, except for inclusion of brief quotations with attribution in a review or report. Requests for reproduction or related information should be addressed to the Contact page at www.badhandbooks.com.

This is a work of fiction. All characters, products, corporations, institutions, and/or entities in this book are either products of the author's imagination or, if real, used fictitiously without intent to describe actual characteristics.

Bad Hand Books
www.badhandbooks.com

For Jessica M

And for Athena:
You were my wolf.

And is that Woman all her crew?
Is that a DEATH? and are there two?
—Samuel Taylor Coleridge

THE WIND BEGAN TO HOWL

PART I
WILHELM SCREAMERS

CHAPTER ONE
(After Avalon)

As autumn slouched closer, my tarot card spread turned up fools, hanged men, and devils. Sycamore leaves had aged a couple of weeks past peak green. Warm, golden afternoons. Evenings were brisk, but a man might've fooled himself with the notion summer would last forever. I had a nice view of the Catskills out the window of my office on the second floor of the Elton Cooper Building in Stone Ridge. A decaying three-story pile of brick and plaster surrounded by forested neighborhoods two blocks north of the hamlet's main drag.

The sign on the frosted glass of the front door read, *Coleridge Investigations*. I'd touched up the austerity of my personal space with regional maps and a yellowed movie poster of Clint Eastwood in *The Eiger Sanction*. So far, no one had gotten the joke. The radio broadcasted New York Giants preseason games. Another sign that winter was shrugging into her fur coat. Now and again, I pulled an all-nighter and slept on the vinyl sofa. Owls hooted among the pines and coyotes yipped in nearby fields. Hunting noises. Rabbits and mice screamed. Death noises. Though a member of the hunting caste, I pondered my own demise more frequently of late.

The universe is fond of sending hints.

Theodora Nowakowski, Ted to her friends, was my office manager/girl Friday. She informed me that Marion Curtis requested a meeting. A tough guy mogul attached to various industries; more important, he represented the long arm of the Hudson Valley underworld. Conman, cutthroat killer, forger of pacts that one couldn't refuse.

The Devil himself.

Year five in New York.

Shut of Alaska and my former career as an enforcer for the Outfit. Engaged to a lovely person and surrogate father to her child. Proprietor of a cozy detective agency. Also, the newly-minted part-owner of a home in High Falls. While not swimming in wealth, neither were wolves prowling around the porch. Occasionally, nefarious types tried to pull me back in to my old life—resident criminal enterprises, such as Curtis and the Albany Syndicate, were loath to let me forget my provenance. I'd offended a corporation or two and a wealthy, politically-

THE WIND BEGAN TO HOWL

connected family over in Western New York idly pined for my scalp. Nothing serious; at least nothing I took seriously. However, the mood of gangsters and industrial kingpins is notoriously changeable, and thus I remained on guard.

The sole fly in the ointment? I'd lost a step, my bones ached when the weather changed, and I suffered occasional perceptual glitches, presumably a result of one too many knocks on the head. Oh, and recurring nightmares. Technicolor surround sound variety. Thus, *flies* in the ointment was more accurate.

Grim introspection plagued my quiet moments; a compulsive self-accounting. I hadn't been a cool kid. An outsider, military brat on the move. Mean and fat. Always scraped up, scowling, fronting. Preoccupied with survival in the manner of a stray animal. How did I go from a melancholic punching bag to a brawling, two-headed monster? How had I metamorphosed into Grendel? The Wolfman? Trudging home from another schoolyard beating, I inhaled piss-stench from an alley and my mind flashed an image of a cave, the lair of some prehistoric beast. Something huge and fanged that brooked zero nonsense. That was it. No real epiphany, no Campbellian inciting event to the Hero's Journey. The cave bear entered my bloodstream without fanfare. The lizard coiled in my hindbrain awakened. Things changed after that duo arrived. Playground humiliation inverted as I swiftly escalated from a kid practicing awkward self-defense to running amok. As an adult, I refined and civilized my predatory instincts. Ambrose Bierce said politeness is the only acceptable hypocrisy. A nice suit and a wad of cash fool people into regarding you in a flattering light. An easy smile and civilty don't hurt. My patrons in the Outfit taught me the finest arts of war are deception and diplomacy. I learned the value of face, an ancient concept that dominates the spectrum of social hierarchies; watchword of princes and paupers alike.

Which brings us to Marion Curtis.

If anybody comprehended the intricacies of "face," Curtis did. I guessed he, too, had been an angry kid whose rage fueled his rise to capo of the Deluca crime family. He owned an apartment in New York, a bachelor pad in Albany, and a main spread near Troy. I was summoned to the Troy digs.

Most gangsters at this stage of the declining Mafia empire stuck to McMansions and the nicer split-level houses in the suburbs. This fella represented old school—big, fancy house with a latter 1960s sense of panache. Swimming pool, skeet range. Lots of glass, lots of lights. Cocaine parties and whores galore. He'd been married, might still be; I'd only met his girlfriend, Wanda. Neither wife nor mistress were in evidence today.

We'd crossed paths frequently since I migrated to the Mid-Hudson Valley. However, it was our mutual love of the silver screen that forged a bond. A few years prior, he'd quietly acquired controlling interest in Star

THE WIND BEGAN TO HOWL

Creek, a production company specializing in indie films. The opportunity to combine business (money laundering) and pleasure had proven irresistible to him. As a fellow movie maven, I empathized with his obsession. Every now and again, he reminded me that casting agents were on the lookout for goons with punchable faces and that I fit the bill to a T.

You might assume possessing oodles of disposable cash to indulge in such a grand hobby would make him a cheerful dude. Alas, it proved otherwise.

Curtis said, "Once upon a time, a slew of likeminded bad guys established a Camelot situation, teaming up to give polite society what for. Except it was maybe the anti-Camelot. Picture the kingdom under the ironshod heel of Mordred and his merry death knights. Went gangbusters. Our crew got fat and happy. Then, grim times descended upon Avalon. We had a falling out, you might say." He stuck a Nat Sherman into the corner of his mouth and lit up. My age, more or less. On the job, he slicked his hair, pancaked his acne scars, wore a tailored suit and smelled of Clive Christian. Carried an automatic. Today, he loafed, raccoon-eyed. His paunch bulged from a purple velvet robe. Bronze dragon stitched across the shoulders.

I said, "In the pulp era, detectives were unscrupulous. They relied upon casual violence. Tarnished knights. Ronin. Gunfighters. That's me."

"You got thrown out of your Camelot." He took

delight in needling me about my downfall with the Outfit.

"I got thrown out of Avalon."

It pleased me to see him, in a morbid sense. We were frenemies, as the kids say. One aspect of several I missed in regard to the mob? The almost enforced camaraderie. Be it busting heads, recovering property, or eating dinner, you seldom lacked for company of like-minded people. A true fellowship. At least until somebody was ordered to stab an icepick into somebody else's eyeball.

Curtis said, "Speaking of tarnished knights and exiles. I once employed a former detective with NYPD. Quit the job early. Drank too much and beat his wife too often, even for them. Got busted for stealing boxes of cards at weddings. Shitheel walked in bold as brass, ate the shrimp cocktails, drank the champagne, kissed the brides and the brides' mothers. Pulled it off for three or four years, too. Lost everything and did a stretch."

"Your type of guy," I said.

"Oh, verily. Until he ate one calzone too many and his heart seized. Real pity. He was my Bruno Le Noir. Once a cop always a cop. Knew all their angles by heart."

"Turncoat is an important role."

"You would know from Bruno."

"Or the Black Knight. I sure as hell wasn't Gawain or Percival."

"Fuckin' pansies, those two. And now?"

I tasted the scotch. Old and strong.

"I was the guy who tracked down the innocent witness and made him and his testimony vanish at the behest of the prime movers. Now I'm the guy who protects the witness and makes sure dirty linen sees the light of day."

"Redemption? You believe in such horseshit?"

"I believe in redemptive acts and sandcastles, both of which amount to nothing, but assuage the emotional necessity to fill space with action."

He blinked, then shook his head, negating my words.

"Kingsnake is your alter ego. The snake kills venomous snakes."

"Don't call me a pelican spider, we're cool."

"Sure, it's a deal. You're a rare talent, Isaiah. People think any big, mean dude with no scruples gets phoned up to the major leagues. We know it's more complex. A successful enforcer possesses a suite of talents to complement physical gifts and natural ferocity. A pro has to drink boiling water and piss ice cubes. He's got to be ruthless, tireless, and he's got to be beloved of the gods. Has to act like he doesn't have vitals to stab."

I patted my midsection through my jacket. I'd dressed casually in a linen shirt, slacks, and tennis shoes. You don't show up a capo in his parlor.

"My vitals are secure. Yours too. As for forbidding times and the decline of civilization...When people wring their hands about some garbage perpetrated by their fellow man, I wonder if they've cracked a single history book. We've always lived in dark times. We invented them."

"Indeed, we did. You're older and more hobbled every time we meet, Coleridge. Crows' feet and gray hairs. The life seeping from your pores. I'd swear you got married. Made any progress on your bucket list?"

"To keep my nose clean."

He chuckled.

"Yeah? And I wanna job artfully sprinkling sand on the asses of bikini models. I think we're destined to perish with our life's ambitions unfulfilled. Wanna hear my great regret?"

"That you were born in the wrong century? You aren't a medieval potentate and can't kill everybody who gives you static?"

"Try me. Nah, my lament is spending thirty-two years on the ladder, bumping off fools as I climbed, pulling cons, arranging heists, the fun stuff, and what those promotions earned me in the end is, well..." He thrust his chin at the house. "Now I'm chained to a desk in my office, yakking on the phone to film distributors, vending machine sales reps, and flunkies out the wazoo. The spark has died."

"Real sorry you're bored and rich," I said. "Plenty of regular Joes would kill to switch places with a guy who lives like a king off the vending machine racket and counting box office receipts."

"Worse than boredom. The Family is dying off, my friend. Defanged, deballed, domesticated. Gone

THE WIND BEGAN TO HOWL

the way of the Yakuza, shingles hanging in front of our offices. The Feds hardly bother to tap our phones or tail us anymore. Sure, sure, you call vending machines a racket. Sadly, it and my Star Creek venture are straight legit businesses. This comes to the point of our meeting. There's a snag with one of my film projects. I need a solid."

"Marion, I don't loan my neighbor tools and I don't owe you or Albany any favors. Down that road lies ruin."

He blew a smoke ring, unfazed.

"Our mutual associate, Gil Finlay, is the one who needs the favor. Some legal snafu with his new film, *The Wind Began to Howl*."

"Catchy," I said.

"Now listen: I don't care whether you can make him happy. Just put in an appearance. Get him and the lawyers off my ass."

"Again…"

"Did I say favor? My bad. Call it a request."

"Totally different story. I do requests."

CHAPTER TWO
(Howl)

Somewhere in the wild Catskills there's a tavern named The Fisherman. Sits upon a hill on a lonely backroad. Could've been a stop for royal coaches and highwaymen in another time. Fossilized timber walls, a shake roof and sparrow nests. Dim, rustic interior. Boar head nailed to the wall, Tanya Tucker and Lead Belly on the jukebox.

Gil Finlay picked it for our Midsummer Eve rendezvous. He was on vacation, unwinding before the post-production slog of *The Wind Began to Howl.* You might've heard of him as director of the nihilistic masterpiece shocker, *The Ornithologist,* which put the brakes on his career, or its follow-up, the surprise Cannes darling, *Torn Between Two Phantom Lovers,* which resurrected it. Some might argue that shooting a mockumentary about the enduring tragedy of the so-called Suicide Forest of Japan was in poor taste, but what can you do with an American "auteur," right?

Gil and I were acquainted these past couple of years primarily because of our overlapping social circles. Curtis informed him I was a fellow one stored in his rolodex for a rainy day. We'd kibitzed at parties, waxing poetic over a mutual adoration of Clark Ashton Smith and Kurosawa. Tonight was our first meeting in my official capacity.

I arrived near sundown and found him at a corner table, studying his phone. Stocky. Middle-aged white boy. Buzzcut, jeans, and a Star Wars T. He was unlike the show biz types I'd met while breaking skulls for the Outfit; not Hollywood at all. More of an erudite comics nerd who somebody occasionally handed a bag of cash to make an arthouse flick. He appeared perpetually bemused by his good fortune.

"Thanks for coming, dude."

"Curtis says you should be my priority." I glanced around. "Where's Rikki?" That would be Gil's wife and publicist.

"We rented an Air BnB down the road. She's catching up on *Unsolved Mysteries.* Says hi."

"The world isn't the same without Robert Stack." I ordered a steak sandwich, potato salad, and a stout beer. "Enjoying the new property?"

He'd bought a spread ten minutes north of my Stone Ridge office last year. Big house. Trees, fields, a creek. All that jazz.

"Should have Norman Rockwell and Thoreau for drinks. But we're over it." His hands moved to illustrate his words.

THE WIND BEGAN TO HOWL

"Problems in paradise?"

The waitress brought him another iced tea. He glanced out the window where red sunset had given way to the sludgy glow of a streetlamp.

"Dude, the house is fucked up."

"That covers a lot of ground. How so?"

"Haunted."

"What's Rikki think?"

"She thinks it's haunted."

"Haunted houses aren't my specialty."

"Screw living in the Amityville manor. We listed the property and moved our shit back to Providence already. Problem solved."

"Because if you want an exorcist, I can put you in touch with a guy used to work for the Vatican…"

He smiled faintly.

"I *want* to hire you to track a couple of weirdos. The Barnhouse brothers. Band name is The Barnhouse Effect. Familiar with their work?"

"Recording artists. Curtis was vague…"

"Cult legends. They're in the wind. Figured this is your forte."

"We'll see. Tell me what happened."

"No drama. I borrowed the heart of a funky composition of theirs, "Boötes & 68," for the score in my new film. Forty-one seconds. Of course, I requested permission."

I ran a search on my phone and located an audio file of the song. Played a few bars. Philip Glass on drugs mixed with strains of electronica. Some

25

unnerving texture rumbling beneath the surface beat. Melancholic and spooky.

"Trippy. I dig it."

"You're not getting half the effect without subwoofers."

The server returned with my sandwich and a fresh bottle of beer.

Gil laid out the case while I demolished supper.

"The Barnhouses are based in Saugerties. We're friendly. Partied hardy, you might say. A few years back, I was dinking around with a script influenced by their aesthetic. Wanted to include part of a song and made my ask. They said okay, dude. Everything seemed cool. Time goes by, I finish the script. More time passes, I rewrite the fucking thing, pitch it, and holy shit, it gets made. Filming wraps, I start the hardcore edits. Keep in mind, it's been an age since I first casually made my request to the Barnhouses. Now, brutal reality slaps me in the kisser. Studio requires a contract for the music sample. Lawyers drew up the boilerplate—"

"Who's handling it?"

"An outside firm we use frequently. Clupach, Ransom, and Friend. Headquartered upstate."

"Yeah, never heard of them. Continue."

"Since the Barnhouses released the album independently, it should be a formality. The road to true love is a winding bitch. The brothers flaked. Been three months since anybody's seen hide or hair. I visited their condo. Locked tight, newspapers on the porch. Their ride was gone."

THE WIND BEGAN TO HOWL

"Make, model."

"Uh, 1970s or '80s Ford van. Black and red. A shaggin' wagon."

"A shaggin' wagon?"

"Yeah, man. I spoke to people in the area. Neighbors didn't know anything and didn't care. Happy not to hear music through the walls at oh-my-God-in the morning. I even got desperate enough to try the police department. Cops aren't searching. Guess the boys have a history. There's the Cliffs Notes."

"Known addresses," I said. "Contact info. Names of friends and close associates. My office manager will combine your info with our database and see what shakes loose."

"Figured. I put together a dossier." He squinted at his phone and tapped the screen. "On its way. Sorry, it's really thin. So's you know, I tried the obvious route—researched their label and producer, mutual friends, et cetera. People ignored me or gave me the ol' runaround. Now, the clock is ticking."

"Have the contract with you?"

"The contract? No. It's…" He smacked his head. "I'll have a copy ready soonest. Hey, could you and Meg swing by next weekend? We're throwing a shindig for the crew and friends of the film. I'm grilling. Bring Robard—Rikki loves him."

Everybody loved Lionel or wanted to smash his face in. Sometimes it wasn't a zero-sum game.

"Not one to turn down a burger and neither is

Lionel. Any chance your boys left the country? No overseas adventures unless my retainer gets a lot fatter."

"Understood. I'm fattening the retainer anyhow. It's on corporate's tab."

"Good. Put my sandwich on their tab, too. Gil, I don't understand—why not edit the score? Wouldn't it be way easier to slot in new music rather than roll the dice on a snipe hunt?"

Fervor kindled in his eyes.

"Easier? One hundred percent. Worse comes to worst, that's what I'll do, God help me, I will. Make a run at this and I'll pray to whomever watches over indie filmmakers that my vision remains intact. The Barnhouses' contribution is integral to the mood, the soul. Shake every tree, beat every bush."

Nobody ever said auteurs were sane.

"Talk about them; give me a feel for what I'm dealing with."

"Did I mention they're weird? Soulful, blissful, heads up their asses self-absorbed. I'm a nerd, okay? I'm a square in comparison. They'll run parlor tricks or try to build a backyard radio to signal aliens. Housesit a pot farm. Headline an orgy. Introverted extroverts, like Prince. Born in the '70s, which explains some of their flower power, monster sideburns and pornstar 'stache aesthetic."

"When you last spoke, was everything normal? Anybody hassling them? Did they have a project under deadline? Artists are wont to behave erratically under pressure."

He said, "No pressure, no deadlines. They're semi-retired."

"Okay. Assuming I get a line on these suckers, what do you want me to do with them?"

"We'll pay your day rate to hunt. Actually convince those bozos to sign the contract like they promised? Major bonus."

"Convince them, eh?"

He laughed nervously.

"Desperate times. You gotta put a gun to their heads, you gotta put a gun to their heads."

I said I could do that.

Driving home, I swerved to miss a deer that vaulted into the road. Rebuilt 1959 Ford. New tires, new brakes. Fishtailed briefly, regained control, and made a hard stop. Jarred my fillings. No major damage to the truck besides a dinged rim. An eerie scene with flashers reflecting off black trees and the lumpy country asphalt. I grumbled, flashlight tucked under my chin as I broke out the jack and a spare. My significant other, Meg, would say, *A few inches to the left, Bambi is sitting in your lap. A few inches to the right, you're wrapped around a pine. Count your blessings, honey.* Hypothetical Meg was correct.

I finished swapping tires and stowed my tools. Across the road, amorphous forms solidified right at the edge of the truck's headlight range. Several deer gathered upslope of the ditch. Frozen, glinting eyes fixed upon me. Reminiscent of a medieval tapestry. I wondered if they were real or the ghosts of animals killed by rocketing trucks like mine. Had they gathered to honor my heroic efforts in swerving around a member of the herd? Didn't feel like it. Felt ominous. I recalled the recent story of a local wildlife photographer who'd snapped pics of a doe licking a human corpse for its salt.

The deer watched me climb inside and roar off. I turned on the radio. A preacher man from Central Casting said, *You're a criminal. You'll always be a criminal. You're a demon. You'll always be a demon.*

I clicked it off with a quickness.

CHAPTER THREE
(Cat Party)

On a lazy Saturday afternoon, I strolled Main Street Rosendale with Megara Shaw, light of my life, gazing into shop windows. Her son, Devlin, either raced ahead or lagged behind, mercurial as any typical nine-year-old. Between entrances to a used bookstore and a deli was a narrow door painted solid green. Concealed by weeds, a decrepit stencil sign leaned against the brick wall. Its peeling cursive letters read CAT PARTY: WEEKENDS 4PM-8PM.

"Hmm," Meg said. "Should we?"

"It's getting late," I said. "A cat party might not literally mean a cat party. Feels ominous."

"I keep you around to defuse threatening situations."

We climbed the stairs behind the door. The interior smelled of decayed leaves and wet fur. Devlin was amped at the notion of attending his very first cat party. What do you know? It was exactly as promised: a cat party, held in a narrow room full of antique furniture. Big band music played softly. A gray woman and her college-aged compatriot served tea and cupcakes. The girl's baggy shirt advertised the Broadway classic *CATS!* She introduced us to the starring felines: Zeta, Lomax, Cali, Purr Bear, Bierce, Van Damme, and Harley. The cats preened, lapped tuna off saucers, and batted around catnip-laced toys. Some wore ribbons, another a bonnet. Pretty damned decadent if you asked me.

"Bierce is feral!" the older lady, who didn't comport herself like someone truly in the spirit of the event, warned me as I bent to pet a fluffy Siamese. He hissed and darted under a dresser. Understandable.

"How many are feral?" I said.

"Only the ones you don't see," the lady said. "Plus Bierce."

"There's a whole colony in the woods," her young friend said.

Devlin and I shared a huge wicker chair. We petted the more stoned cats (Zeta and Purr Bear) while Meg snapped a zillion pictures. I drank a dainty cup of tea and ate a cupcake. Then I stuffed a few bucks in a jar labeled SUPPORT THE CATHOUSE. We returned home covered in cat hair.

Meg had quit her library job shortly after we bought the house in High Falls—1970s split level; picket fence in the front; enchanted forest out back. Half a dozen other homes down the lane. A deer or possum in every yard. Which is to say, typical Hudson Valley rural neighborhood.

The High Falls Library needed a director. And no, I didn't bump the fellow off to pave the way, regardless of my eminent qualifications to do so. Cons: longer hours, more responsibility. Pros: close to home and a significant pay hike. Meg accepted the gig. Months later, she worried how her choice might affect Devlin. Juggling domestic obligations was rough, especially with school out. Currently, he attended an activities program with several classmates. This reduced the pressure.

"I'll take in the slack," I said, doggedly jamming a pile of breakfast dishes into the washer.

"Take in the slack how?" She stood at the window, watching the boy toss sticks for my dog, Minerva, in the back yard. "Grass is knee-high to a giraffe…" The light gathered in her dark hair and she stole my breath.

"If you get in a bind, I'll take a shift. No worries." We weren't married; hard to say whether we'd ever get there. I nonetheless tried to shoulder the role of father figure to her son. The role wasn't a natural fit.

"When, love? Your schedule is wack."

"Wack?"

"Eccentric as Mercury's orbit, I meant."

"It's been crazy at the office. Keep saying I'll hire

another body. Maybe it's time. Past time. I'm sorry about the grass."

"Evil never rests."

I prevailed against the washer door and was feeling confident.

"He can do a ride-along. Surefire bonding activity."

"Oh my God." Meg turned to regard me. "Yep, you're serious." She walked over, reached up and cupped my face. Lavender lotion on her skin. "No, my love, you're not taking Devlin on a stakeout of some den of iniquity—"

"Car dealer gets in a honey trap at the Lost Weekend Motor Inn. Photos to the wife. High time the boy learned to operate the Nikon."

"—or to help you hang some jerk off a ledge by his ankles—"

"Lionel usually gets the other ankle," I said.

"Don't be a wiseass."

I hugged her and related my confab with Gil and the task he'd set me. Naturally, I elided mention of Curtis. I was the only (ex) gangster she tolerated.

"Rock stars?" she said. "And they're missing."

"Hard to find, at any rate."

"Anybody file a missing-persons report?"

"Meg, they're not missing, they're—"

"—hard to find. I hear you. Wouldn't it be nice?" Her smile was wistful.

"To be hounded by a goon to sign the Devil's contract? Doesn't sound nice. Sounds stressful."

"Honey, you've been demoted from a goon. You're a lug."

The next couple of days involved the usual routine of such a case: Ted conducted background checks and sifted social media for intel on the Barnhouses and anyone in their orbit. Referencing Gil's notes, I contacted a handful of industry pros who'd set up for the brothers or backed them at concerts. Parents were deceased and the other relatives proved forthcoming as turnips. What I gleaned: born in the Pacific Northwest and raised on a remote farm. Spent their teens in New York State. Both served in the US Army; Roger had seen action in the Persian Gulf. Later, enrolled at the University of Washington and graduated two years apart in the mid to latter '90s. They burrowed into the Seattle underground arts scene, gained a respectable following, and then migrated back to New York. Initiated weird recording projects, culminating in four albums stretching between 2003 and 2013. They also coauthored three decidedly mid-list literary thriller novels before the New York publisher cut them loose. Their assorted jacket photos were hardcore retro—shaggy hair, 1776 sideburns, and beards. Akin to the likes of Steely Dan, Gordon Lightfoot, and the Allman Brothers. This didn't move me closer to finding them, although it sure established a mood. Ken was blondish; Roger was seven feet tall, according to the bio.

An item in the catalogue of digital press clippings, interviews, and articles struck me as particularly interesting: an arts and culture magazine had done a human-interest piece in 1998 about a team of geologists exploring caves in Mexico. One color photo, slightly unfocused and marred by lens flares featured the very young Barnhouses posed with a dozen other explorers at the bottom of a huge cavern. Hardhats and overalls. Sweaty, dirt-streaked faces. Smiling. Quartz deposits and glaciers of crystal bounced dazzling hot lamp beams everywhere. The Barnhouses were briefly referenced as "folk rock musicians contributing to acoustic tests." Ken Barnhouse was quoted as saying he and his brother were neophyte spelunkers, fascinated with the notion of how harmonics are amplified and "recorded" by certain minerals.

No jackpot in the database meant resorting to actual legwork. Legwork goes faster with good company. Besides a faithful hound, Lionel Robard was about the best company a man could ask for. He lived in a cabin on Hawk Mountain Farm; a sprawling, ramshackle commune located in the woods between New Paltz and Rosendale. Established during the 1960s by flower power advocates, the property represented safe harbor for lame horses, old dogs, new age druids, and other lost souls. I had a soft spot in my calcified heart for the elderly owners—I'd searched for the missing granddaughter. My unofficial debut case, ending in tragedy that bonded us forevermore.

THE WIND BEGAN TO HOWL

Lionel was a few years younger than me, which didn't make him a spring chicken. Ex-military. Lean and scruffy. Fond of his Australian drover hat, Carhartt jacket, jeans, and hiking boots. Amber-tinted shooting glasses, depending upon how much he'd drunk the night before. He dressed more snappily on special occasions, which I credited to my influence. Dyed-in-the-wool ladies' man, smitten with a corporate heiress named Delia Labrador. Wicked Delia toyed with his affections, to my dismay. Currently, she gallivanted across Europe in the company of other filthy rich ne'er-do-wells. Lionel was also smitten by cigarettes and cheap beer. He mended fences at the farm, kept the equipment running, and pitched hay as required. Handy with guns and knives and not too shabby as a driver. If I needed backup on a job, I paid him a visit. Sometimes I called on him when I was lonesome after too many solo stakeouts.

This marked such a day.

He wasn't repairing the moribund tractor or shoveling manure, however. Instead, he'd gotten into some sort of territorial pissing contest with contractors from an adjacent farm. So much for peace and love. The contractors were a fly-by-night outfit, given to off-roading across private property, littering, spooking the horses, and such. The epitome of brewing trouble. Lionel and a thick-necked, beer-bellied lunk were squared up in a pasture on the fence line. Both had stripped to their T-shirts. Several guys stood around talking trash. Money changed hands. Nothing like a squabble among hungover, bellicose peasantry to liven up the dreary workaday routine.

"Aight, hayseed. Aight." Barrel Gut spat and bounced, settling into a caricature of *Raging Bull*, thumbs sticking out from his blocky fists. I wondered which one Lionel would snap first.

I asked a young laborer what the two were fighting over. The kid pointed to a sprung section of barbed wire. The contractor and his boys had snipped it with wire cutters to forge an illicit shortcut.

"Hold up." I stood next to Lionel. "Amigo, you want to borrow my knucks?" I carried a set of brass knuckles under the seat of my Ford alongside a hunting knife, a jade war club, and a med kit. Tools for every job.

"Get back to you after I sock him a couple of times."

I lowered my voice.

"He has stubby T-rex arms and forty pounds on you. He'll try to lunge in and maul, so keep a check hook ready. Circle left and pop him with your jab. Can't hurt him, but he won't like it. Bust his nose as soon as possible, shut down his breathing. Smack his ear."

"Smack his ear? That gonna mess with his breathing too?"

"No. It'll be hilarious, though."

Lionel's left arm crossed his stomach. He hunched,

chin to chest, looking everywhere but at his foe. His right fist rested against his temple. I smiled to recognize the Philly Shell. Aging guys like us appreciated the classics.

Somebody clapped twice to signal time in. Barrel Gut and Lionel got cracking. Incidentally, it was the left thumb.

We clattered down the dirt road toward the highway.

"That'll teach him not to trespass on Hawk Mountain land." Lionel fanned himself with the drover hat and pressed an ice-cold Busch tallboy against his swollen eye. He'd cleaned up and put on a fresh, unbloodied shirt. Combing his hair didn't alter the impression he'd gotten walloped with a pillowcase full of padlocks.

"Allow me to introduce you to the term, Pyrrhic victory," I said.

"Victory is victory. Spared him a load of buckshot. Saving people is harder than destroying them."

"Been talking to Meg, I see."

He popped the top on his beer.

"I'm worried for you. You're off-kilter. Getting soft in the wrong ways."

His observation jolted me. Lionel had a knack for dialing into my frequency. I throw to the Māori on

Mom's side of the family. Tallish, darkish, and thickish. I'd shed a few stubborn pounds. Some would say I could've stood to shed a few more. He wasn't referring to my dad bod, though. He meant the brooding, the anxious introspection.

I tried to laugh it off.

"Really? Hell, last night I spent a solid five minutes itemizing all the ways I have it good."

"Hey, I don't mean to overstep. My radar is getting pinged, all I'm saying."

"Gray hairs." I rubbed my jaw. "Arthritis. Shrinking bladder. Bifocals. I'm in decline."

"Gibbon will be penning your bio at this rate. I'm worried about them ghosts crawling around in your head. Man has steady nightmares the way you do, he's cracking. Trust me." He seldom spoke of his time in Afghanistan. Plainly, it had a profound effect upon him, one that became more pronounced as years rolled by.

"You *have* been talking to Meg."

"What's the deal? They scanned your brain and results were clean."

"Doctors didn't pronounce me clean." I'd had a CAT scan after a nasty blow to the dome a couple of years prior. Getting conked over the head was an occupational hazard. I'd made peace with it. Occasionally, I suffered glitches—hallucinations, lost time, et cetera. "They didn't find anything. The veritable distinction between innocent and not guilty."

"Cancer?" He tossed the empty, pulled a cigarette from behind his ear, and struck a match.

I rolled onto the highway, heading north.

In the olden days, a leech would declare I suffered ill humors, chronic ague, or an infestation of evil spirits. The leech, like any stopped clock, would be correct. Father Time was closing in. To stave him off, I lifted, jogged rugged Shawangunk trails, and put in time grappling with the boys down at the Deadfall gym. Over the past few months. I'd gone rounds as a local heavyweight's sparring partner. The kid, huge, monstrously strong, and mean, had gone through a bunch of partners. None were eager to get mangled again for love or money. The rising star merely needed a big, durable stiff to punch and strangle. I'm not a highly skilled mixed martial artist, but that I could do.

"Not cancer, right?" Once Lionel latched on, he seldom relented.

"It's indefinable."

"Cancer?"

"Yo, homie. I'm not the two-pack-a-day fool in this cab."

This quip bought me a minute of silence.

"Nietzsche was full of shit," he said at last. "Suffering doesn't make you stronger. For an oak, every fresh tragedy is an axe blow."

CHAPTER FOUR
(Kolchak and the Psychopomps)

Of all the places I've lived, New York State is the loveliest. Wilderness lurks off every garden path in the Rondout Valley. The short ride to Kingston on this sweet midmorning in August was like driving into the cover of a vintage *Field & Stream.*

Alas, US cities are inevitably cities, which is to say piles of metal and concrete. I parked in a rear lot on the not-so-green west side. Radio station WZXY sat at the end of a row featuring a Mexican restaurant and a pawn shop. The Mexican joint made terrific enchiladas. I'd brought Devlin there for his last couple of birthday dinners. Kid swore by it. We walked around front. Somebody had propped open the station's dented security door with a brick. Leaves, candy wrappers, and dirt swirled around the carpet in the deserted reception area. Thin, aquarium light seeped under blinds. Smelled musty as hell. Recorded voices droned nearby. Put me in mind of priests or warlocks reciting incantations.

"What am I doing here?" Lionel fidgeted. "Tractor ain't gonna fix itself."

"Neither will you. It's good to ditch the farm." And, as he prepared a retort, I said, "The Golden Eel and Billy Bob's Liquor Emporium don't count."

"Tee-hee. Seriously, though."

"Look around. Place gives me the willies. Thank God I didn't come here alone. Might vanish mysteriously."

A balding man appeared in a doorway and beckoned. Judd Aker, program director. An inveterate gambler who frequently got himself in Dutch with the friendly neighborhood loan sharks. I'd saved his bacon on behalf of my mobster acquaintances in Albany— Aker dated the second cousin of some wiseguy. Herr Program Director and I weren't on the friendliest of terms despite my saving his bacon. Prideful type. Nonetheless, his name was in the Barnhouse dossier and when I redeem a marker, even a knucklehead like him honors the debt.

He sat behind a metal desk. A photo hung over his shoulder; De Niro as Capone smoking a cigar. Tiny window with the blinds snugged, same as every other window in the joint. Clock permanently stopped at half-past four. That was it.

"These window sills lined with garlic?" Lionel said. "Because the villagers at the inn insist it's a good idea."

"I don't hang around here after the sun goes down, all I'm gonna say." Aker clasped his hands behind his

THE WIND BEGAN TO HOWL

head. Affecting boredom while sneaking glances at me to gauge the weather. Thunderheads massing. "Tough sledding for a radio broadcaster."

"Count your lucky stars you didn't grow up to be a newspaper man," I said.

"*Kolchak the Night Stalker* wept," Lionel said.

Aker didn't get the reference. Likely too young to have indulged in late-night 1970s television.

"The Barnhouse Effect," I said. "Regular theremin virtuosos. Their music was in rotation in the Mid-Hudson market, thanks to you."

"Rotation on weekends during the graveyard stretch," Aker said. "Same slot for ambient noise, B-side house music, and the lamentably cancelled Porter's Peculiar Picks Science Fiction Hour."

"More than business associates. Friends?"

"Friendly, not friends," he said. "C'mon, big fella, I told Finlay this shit already. Important part of my job is to scope the regional scene for the comers. Nobody in the wider world gives a rat's ass. The Barnhouses are low-key celebrities for this area, though. Roger is the brains of the band. He negotiated with a cheapskate label for their first three albums. I stepped in and hosted a get-together for their sophomore record release. Another role of mine is shepherding talent. Be it spinning their LPs, gratis publicity, or making C-listers feel like A-list celebrities."

"The record label was too stingy for an L.A. party?" I said.

"L.A. party? Pterosaur Records is too cheap to throw a Kerhonkson party in a cornfield. Life moves fast in La-La Land. The bloodsuckers at Pterosaur forgot they'd signed those poor chumps in the first place and regretted the gesture once somebody in accounting reminded them." Aker was into his narrative; his voice an octave this side of strident. He said *La-La Land* in the tone of a disaffected functionary exiled from the bright city lights to pushing pencils at a gulag. "Wasn't gonna rain on the parade, y'know? I sprang for the whole deal and let Ken and Roger assume the execs kicked in."

"Very sweet. Happen to see them recently?"

"Not since last summer at Hempapalooza." He watched Lionel stand abruptly and walk out. "Uh, your buddy. Leon—"

"Lionel," I said as the door shut.

"I bore him? Can't just wander the halls…"

"He's probably snooping." I waved Aker back into his chair. "You were telling me where to find the Barnhouse twins."

"They aren't twins." He scowled at the door. "Snooping for what? Nothing to find. It's a radio station."

"Hell if I know. Could be anything. A pallet of cocaine. Hookers chained in the boiler room. Don't worry; he's discreet. But we're off topic. Any idea where the Barnhouses hang out and whom with?"

"Coulda done this on the phone. 'I have no fucking clue' takes like three seconds, tops."

"And deprive myself of the pleasure of slamming your fingers in a filing cabinet? Try checking your records. Since I drove all this way and whatnot."

"Surely I'm not the only miserable fucker who broke bread with these dudes."

"True. You're not Mr. Right, you're Mr. Right Now. Tomorrow, I'll be hassling somebody else." I flashed him one of my meaner smiles from the old days when I'd been somebody else.

It achieved the desired effect. Aker sullenly reached into his desk. Conjured a memo pad and theatrically flipped pages. I'd considered the possibility he was going for a gun. The dude had been strong-armed and was head shy; reasonable to assume he kept a piece handy.

"Okay, I can point you in the general direction." He scribbled, then tore out a page and pushed it toward me. "Record label dissolved. Cordell Harms produces their albums. He splits time between the Apple and his office in L.A. Travels the world at the drop of hat. Producers think they're royalty. Have fun. Then you got an ex-girlfriend. Krystal Niven. She lives here in town."

"Whose ex?"

"Pick 'em. Wildcat."

"Noted."

"Gotta be straight, she won't talk to you. She's a hard-nosed bitch when it comes to her boys."

"Also noted," I said.

"Last name on there is Tod Lyra. Phone number might not be legit. Weird, weird dude. Simpatico with the Barnhouses. He's...well, you'll see."

"Lyra's the drug hookup, huh?"

"Why did you leap to that conclusion?"

"The twinkle in your eye." I'd heard of Lyra in passing as a consequence of traveling in the same seedy circles. Small-time dealer to small-time stars and wannabes. He specialized in the softer side of vice—grass, pills, and hallucinogens.

"He's a regular at the Debonair," Aker said.

"See, you did have a clue."

Back in the truck, I asked Lionel where he'd gone during the interview.

"Your buddy is a Renfield type. A minion. I searched for the crypt."

"The crypt?"

"Yeah, where the vampire lord sleeps."

"I'm confiscating your comic books," I said. "Radio stations don't normally feature crypts in the floorplan."

"Normally," Lionel said. "Actually, I was looking for the head. Needed to vent some beer. Couldn't find one anywhere."

"Oh, we'll make a pitstop."

"No need. I took care of it."

I nonetheless detoured into a Jamaican deli and bought a couple of boxes of fried chicken, home fries, coleslaw, and Cokes. We sat in a deserted lot near the river and ate lunch. An elderly man in a wide-brimmed fishing hat leaned against a shopping cart piled with plastic bags. He chucked tidbits of bread and the gathered seagulls squabbled to be first.

After a while, I buzzed the music producer in California, Cordell Harms, and left a voice message. His name pinged in a few spots on an internet search, but nothing current. Dartmouth grad whose vague work history included the State Department, consulting firms, and two major record labels. His most recent photo was out of date—late '50s, thinning hair gelled over his left eye in a gothic swoop, mild features, easy smile. Could've been a mensch or a cannibal. Next, I tried the ex-girlfriend, Krystal Niven. Rang to voicemail, but she broke in halfway through the message. Asked what I wanted in a tone colder and deader than the voicemail robot.

"Hi, Krystal. I'm Isaiah, friend of Ken and Roger. Maybe you recall meeting me a few years back at one of Judd Aker's shindigs? The guys and I jammed together and I'm hoping to get in touch."

"Fuck yourself." She hung up.

Lionel tossed the bones into the box. He wiped his fingers and lit a cigarette.

"Speaking of dreams."

"We weren't," I said.

"Earlier, on the way into town."

"Right."

He shook the box of chicken bones near his ear as though tapping into the oracular power of an animist tradition. He professed a steadfast conviction that rocks and trees absorbed the echoes of time and energy. Motionless in a deer blind as a kid in the west, and again in the high deserts of Afghanistan as a Marine Corps sniper, he'd learned the secret language of the wilderness. Or so he raved at me one night as I lugged him out of the bar in a fireman's carry.

"Was recently smote by a vision," he said. "A doozy. Astral projected right out of my body. Sort of a religious experience that sheds a ray of light on your situation. I had to take a piss in the middle of the night—"

"I detect a theme."

"Might've been wasted. Tripped and landed on the coffee table. Split my head under the hairline. Knocked me unconscious."

"Jesus, Lionel." Considering how often I'd had my own skull dented while pursuing various misadventures, I wasn't in any position to judge.

"After the shooting stars fizzle and the tweety birds stop chirping, I have a dream. Crystal clear, technicolor. I'm on a stage, spotlight beaming down. This choir of, I dunno, angels, descends. Psychopomps might be another term. Sorta hokey, sorta terrifying. Their visages are white and rubbery as masks. They murmur in my mind. *You will bear witness.* And I zip through time and space until I'm levitating a few feet above the ocean. Cold and choppy, but I'm a ghost. Then this 747 roars out of the mist, skims the water, and tips portside and bursts. Huge, dirty waves smash over the wreckage. Doesn't matter. I see everything. Rows of seats and luggage and people hurled into the air before the wave smashes them under. In my ear, *You will bear witness.* The crash replays. *You will bear witness.* Then again and again. *You will bear witness.* Faster each time. *You will bear witness.* They rewind the tape. I scream—" He wiped sweat from his forehead. "Woke up, hair matted in blood. Skull hurting. Waking is the wrong idea—more like I dropped into my body. Couldn't shake it for days. Still haven't."

"Definitely a vision," I said.

"Make a true believer of you yet."

"My skepticism is increasingly tempered by our experiences. Do visions always manifest as reality? No. Does the subconscious apprehend radio signals transmitted by the numinous overmind? Yep."

"Spirituality is fine, but you're not getting religion on my watch. Gotta draw the line there."

"Like I'm not getting cancer."

He cracked another beer without comment.

"Deism isn't my bag," I said. "Yet, more and more, I feel the need to believe in something larger than myself. Hell of an impulse to reconcile."

"True that, brother. Despair starts one night at a listening post as the tickle of a chilly breeze on your neck. Then it's whistling in the caverns of your chest. It becomes too late in a hurry. What about you? Any dreams of note?"

Dear dead Mom believed in the oracular nature of dreams. Her immediate family had lived close to the bone on Aotearoa, and maintained folk traditions. I would've asked her insight into my recurring nightmares. Scant daylight existed between memories of my long-dead Achilles as a pup or his absence which had now grown into a couple of decades. The dog haunted me, racing over the tundra faster than I could chase. Other nights I raced naked and clutching a spear under an apple-green heaven. Sometimes in ancient New Zealand, sometimes Africa. Moa birds churning plains dust. Lions stalking through tall grass, wizened faces swaying.

"No," I said.

CHAPTER FIVE
(Black & Blue Dancing Queen)

For much of the colonial era into modern times, Kingston served as a hub of commerce and transportation. Coal, textiles, cement—the city made or shipped it. More recently, tech giant IBM came and went; first enriching the locals with boomtown fortune, only to abandon them after a handful of decades. Downtown Kingston remained vibrant, especially at its heart, the Stockade district. A web of bistros, coffee shops, and lounges sparkled at night. But the edges of town showed signs of decay. Places like radio station WXZY and surrounding empty lots and abandoned buildings beside the sluggish Hudson. Meanwhile, in the middle distance, the primeval mountains abided, patiently waiting to reclaim the world.

The Debonair began life as a clothing factory in the 1920s and closed its doors in the early '50s. Reminiscent of a lifecycle in other cities, a long period of dormancy was followed by real estate speculation and revival. Investors discovered large, shuttered buildings made excellent discotheques and night clubs. The majority of these had since risen and declined. The Debonair persisted, like those weeds cracking the sidewalk. A belligerent survivor.

The number Aker scribbled actually worked. Tod Lyra answered on the second ring and agreed to meet me after 10 P.M. at the club. I wasn't sure whether that was good or bad.

Off to the Debonair Lionel and I galumphed.

The beefy Samoan doorman was a regular at my gym cum dojo. He twisted me into a pretzel on a weekly basis. I slipped him a few bucks. He stamped our hands and waved us in before a cluster of indignant boys and girls decked out in their meat market finery. To be fair, I wear a suit well. Meg opined it enhanced my "thiccness." Lionel had dressed to impress in a swooping V-neck silk shirt, disco pants, and cowboy boots.

Techno/Industrial Night meant smoggy gloom punctuated by splashes of fire. Booming bass. Eight-dollar well drinks and a hell of a crowd for midweek. I snagged a table near the main dance floor and ordered a Bloody Mary. Lionel did three tequila shots, which I paid for. We drank standing because there weren't any chairs. He saluted me and strutted onto the dance floor as Ministry's "Stigmata" kicked into high gear. Lionel could dance. Had to admit, he was sort of beautiful; black and blue and angelic under the

THE WIND BEGAN TO HOWL

shifting spotlights. Two women drifted into his orbit like metal drawn toward a magnet. Then a dude and a dude's date, and it was the beginnings of an episode of *American Bandstand.*

I tipped the server and ordered another drink. Pixie in a plastic skirt. She returned and said mintily into my ear to follow her upstairs to the VIP lounge. The lounge was a spartan collection of recessed alcoves and amphitheater style central tables with chemical stick lighting. Moody on any other night but tonight.

Lyra's table overlooked the dancefloor. '40s; reedy and angular with a Caesar cut. Rolled sleeves on a plaid button-up shirt. Gold chain, silver bracelet. Sipping a Cosmo in the company of several casually dressed young people. None were muscle. He saw me on the stairs and gestured. I knew he'd reek of hashish and foreign cologne before I got close enough to confirm.

"Here's the killer," Lyra said to his friends with a smirk. Pronounced it kill-uh. Obviously, Aker had relayed a warning about my character. Should've warned him harder. "Straight up killer, no joke. Dude whacked people for the mob." The kids were not impressed. "Howya doing, Killer?"

"I was also the boss' inquisitor. A witchfinder general, if you will."

"Yeah?"

"Ask me, what's the most efficient interrogation method?"

"Okay. What is it?" He sneered; a real hardcase. "Wait, wait—thumbscrews? The rack? Red-hot tongs?"

"Intermittent suffocation." I pushed aside a surprised blonde and squeezed in cozily next to the King. Draped my arm over his shoulders.

It visibly dawned on Lyra he might have poked the wrong bear.

"Inter-what?"

I clamped his nose and mouth with my free hand. Happened fast. I let him struggle a few seconds, then released my grip and had a swallow of his drink. He sagged in shock. The courtiers were stunned too.

I said, "Works better with a ball gag and soda foam squirted up the nose. Plastic bag over the head is another standby. Catch the nightly news? You're familiar with waterboarding. Two minutes with cheesecloth and a bottle of water, I'll get it sorted."

"Tod—" the blonde lost her nerve as she met my bloodshot eye.

Lyra blinked tears. Blood dripped from his nostril. We all sat frozen in time as the music thumped. It could've gone in a number of directions. Lyra chose wisely.

"I came off like an asshole. Apologies." He waved for his court to take a powder, which they happily did. He squirmed away from me and dabbed his nose with a napkin. "In other news, your buddy sure can shake it, huh?"

THE WIND BEGAN TO HOWL

I glanced down where Lionel had attracted a couple more hotties who were ready to climb him like a jungle gym.

"He can cut a rug. I keep him around as a distraction."

"Aker said you're hunting for the Barnhouses."

"Aker tell you why?"

"Contract dispute over music," he said. "Finlay's upcoming flick. His movies are fabulous. Ever catch *The Ornithologist?* Change your life."

"Terrific. Where can I find the boys?"

"No idea."

"Climb into a hole and pull a rock over it. Your dealer will know exactly where you dug that hole."

He chuckled. His flush slowly faded.

"True, true. Hand to God, I haven't personally spoken to those crazy kids since last Halloween. Krystal is who you should corner."

"The ex," I said. "Krystal Niven. She's on my list."

"The main squeeze. Groupies come and go. She always returns. Gonna be a triangle until the day they die. Krystal knows where the boys are, if anybody does. She used to run interference in regard to their, uh, deliveries. Roger's all purple haze up in the joint. Kenneth's a purist. Shrooms. As I said, been a while since I've seen any of them."

"Maybe you could put me in touch with her."

"Get real. Krystal calls me, I don't call her."

"Cordell Harms, their producer?"

"An infamous character. Haven't met him. Let me ask *you* something. Which song did Finlay use?"

"Boötes & 68," I said. "Fifth cut off *The Colossal Nothing*."

"Oh."

"Oh boy? Oh shit? What?"

"Roger studied astronomy," he said. "Ken majored in folklore. Pair of soldier boys; probably attended college on the G.I. Bill because their origins were awfully humble. Fate is twisted; gave those poor fuckers big ol' brains. Too smart to make radio-friendly shit. The entire Barnhouse catalogue alludes to cosmic mysteries. Ken creates vocalizations without equipment I'd swear were impossible if I hadn't heard it myself. Roger is a sleight of hand wiz. Quarter behind your ear, levitation, stupid card gimmicks. Eerie shit, too. They can predict what you have in your pockets, the name of your childhood pets, and what year Aunt Boo died. Walk through walls—and a stunt Roger referred to as seven leagues in one step. An illusion where he walks into a closet and then yells from the front yard five seconds later. People see his silhouette and momentarily grapple with the fact he's beamed himself ninety feet...until he reveals he's still in the closet and somehow projecting his voice while his power of suggestion does the rest. Humans detect what they expect to see and hear. Big hit at the few parties they've attended."

"Wow, you're a hype man. I simply *have* to meet them after this buildup."

He wiped the rim of his glass with his sleeve and sipped.

"The boys don't confide in me. My job is to fill orders. I hear things. What I hear is they followed a wandering star into the hills. Joined a new age cult. Or founded one. Searching for a higher power. Constructing a crystal set to pierce the veil and beam God a prayer. Enslaved themselves to the ineffable mystery, whatever that mystery might be, I haven't the faintest. Sounds nuts, but I say bravo. They weren't the kind to wear three-piece suits, which didn't leave them a fallback position when the music stopped selling. Had to swim away from Alcatraz on their own terms."

"There's not exactly a wealth of biographical information on them. They're prog rock. As in they've gotten progressively weirder with every release."

"We live in crazy times," Lyra said. "Poe described his own existence as madness interrupted by brief, horrible interludes of sanity. Things are more complicated, more toxic. The Barnhouses aren't the kind to withstand modern protocols. Shoulda been a pair of troubadours playing hot festivals during the high medieval era. That weirdness you cite? Old souls harkening to days of yore. It's a cocoon. Roger's fascination with space would've translated as astrology back when. He's far more curious regarding the effects of celestial configurations on human fate than cold equations."

"Witchcraft and Gnosticism triumphed over astrophysics," I said. "Shamans, not scientists."

"Ultimately, it's the same exact proposition. Go hassle Niven. I'm telling you, she's the key."

"Come along, dancing queen." I collected Lionel and headed forth.

He smoked a cigarette in the alley while I put in a call to an associate; a reliable lowlife whose background indicated a tolerance for excruciating boredom. Ted had dug into Krystal Niven's background earlier that day—Niven's spartan social media accounts advertised her as an operations consultant, although details were nebulous. Last known physical address was the Hudson Villa apartment complex on the east side of Kingston, and not close to the river, incidentally. I relayed these basic statistics and bid the lowlife to confirm the lady's whereabouts. Once accomplished, his mission was to hang back and see where she went and whom with.

Lowlife said, "Yeah, I can handle a day shift. Only 'til supper and no Sundays. Church on Sunday."

Football season meant inveterate gamblers chewing their nails to see if the Giants and the Jets beat the spread. Church all right.

"Mind your knitting. Somebody else will cover swing and graveyard." I currently retained half a dozen other freelancers willing to accept day labor gigs if the sole requirements were staying awake and snapping a few pictures.

I keenly hoped one of them would snap something useful.

CHAPTER SIX
(Wilhelm Screamers)

The plot thickened that weekend at Gil and Rikki Finlay's barbecue.

The three-and-a-half-hour drive to Providence became a family affair—Meg at the wheel of her Caravan, Lionel riding shotgun. Devlin, Minerva, and me in back. Devlin confiscated my phone and absorbed himself in some sort of contemporary Tetris update. Minerva stuck her blocky head out the window and left it there. Meg wore the driving gloves and Vivian-Leigh scarf I'd hunted down for her birthday.

Devlin had conducted research on Gil Finlay's directing career. He expressed great interest in screening *The Ornithologist.*

"Isaiah, secure that phone!" Meg said.

"Mom!" Devlin said. "It's about birds. Birds are fascinating. I love them."

"It's rated NC17," I said. "You're gonna get me

killed—back to your game. Don't answer my text messages. And if it rings, hand it over."

"What's NC17?" he said with saccharine innocence.

"Stands for: No Child Is Watching This Shit Until They Go To College," I said.

Lionel said, "I considered Hollywood. Buster Keaton is my spirit animal. Behold these cheekbones. Considered voice acting, too. Cartoons, coffee commercials, and whatnot. Or movie promos: *In a world where—*"

"Always thought you'd do a fantastic Wilhelm Scream," I said.

"Amigo, I had no idea there are copperheads in New York State, much less coiled up in my hat."

"What's a Wilhelm Scream?" Devlin completely forgot about surfing the web.

Meg said, "A high-pitched scream uttered by actors who've been shot off a horse or are ripped apart by hostile fauna."

"Or get punched in the nads." Lionel demonstrated at half volume.

"Cool!" Devlin commenced to practice in my ear.

During a pitstop, I checked in with the Krystal Niven stakeout team. My reliable lowlifes had her in their sights. Gave me a description of her building and car. Apparently, she conducted her consulting business from the apartment, only leaving its comforts to visit a takeout joint and get her hair done at a salon. Boring. Same story with the second shift. Niven stayed put on Thursday. Friday, around 6 P.M., she met a couple of girlfriends for drinks at the Golden Eel—a dive on the Rondout under the 9W bridge. Home alone by 10 P.M. No midnight rendezvous or trips out of town. Again, boring.

I ordered my little hens to keep sitting on their eggs.

Providence emanates a sense of grandeur, of gaslight antiquity. Older streets are sunken and oddly textured; shopfronts crowd the hilly sidewalks. H.P. Lovecraft lived and died in the town where nighttime shadows flow weirdly across the side lanes and back alleys. Criminal elements hold all too much sway, energized by the tension between wealth and poverty. Nonetheless, it's a charmer and those who love Providence love it wholly.

Casa Finlay sat on a quiet block, packed in tight with the other rambling houses. Four stories and vaguely shaped like a barn. Numerous guests gathered in the fenced back yard to drink and observe Gil crisp platters of hotdogs and burgers. Smoke rose above his roaring propane grill and he danced witchily before the flames. Rikki hugged each of us, handed beers to Lionel and me (remarking upon his battered mug), and then absconded with Meg. Devlin was solemnly greeted by young Hamish Finlay, also in fourth grade, and introduced to several other kids who were hanging around. Minerva patrolled, on the alert for dropped crumbs and the Finlays' Maine Coon cat. I knew she'd keep tabs on Devlin.

I was working on my second beer when Gil turned over grilling duties to a production assistant and summoned me and Lionel for a confab under the shady green ash tree. He asked how the case was proceeding, to which Lionel grunted and I shrugged.

"Let me introduce you to one of the guys who drew up the language for the Barnhouses' license." Gil gestured and a thoroughly vanilla white dude in a natty blazer detached from the gaggle and ambled on over. The man shook our hands and smiled blandly. He had the clammy grip of a dead fish. His aftershave was acrid.

"Mr. Coleridge, Mr. Robard. Honored. Bruce Clupach at your service."

"Of Clupach, Ransom, and Friend," I said. "Three of the four riders."

"The same. Our host tells me you're on the trail of our wayward musicians with bloodhound efficiency." Clupach produced a plain envelope. "You'll require this document if and when you happen upon the gentlemen. A piece of advice?" He waited for my nod. "Whatever happens, don't quit. You're an imposing individual. Nonetheless, I must exhort you to be tenacious. Much rides on your success and time is not in abundance."

THE WIND BEGAN TO HOWL

He hesitated. "I trust you'll preserve the sanctity of this document. It may only be unsealed by the lawful recipients upon their stated intent to sign."

"As you say, Bruce."

"Very well. Good health and good fortune to you."

I tucked the envelope inside my jacket.

"Well, thanks. Although I'm sorry you made a trip to Providence just to hand me this piece of paper."

His smile curved toward his sideburns.

"Frankly, our firm is old fashioned. We find merit in pressing the flesh with colleagues, clients, and intermediaries. You pair of cards are infamous. Incidentally, Gil sets a nice spread." He tapped his chin. "As a matter of fact, an old fashioned might hit the spot. Point me the way to the bar."

Watching the back of his oily-slick head drift into the crowd, I was reminded that barring rare exceptions, lawyers and agents gave me the willies.

"There's someone else here you might find interesting," Gil said presently. He'd gulped his share of hard lemonade and was boozily animated. "Recall a foreign science fiction movie in the 1980s...*Synthetic Reflex?* Maybe it was really a horror film with a dystopian setting..."

"Hell, yeah," Lionel said. "1989. Heart of my misspent youth. The poster depicted a buzzsaw-wielding android menacing a topless blonde. False fucking advertising. Nobody shed their clothes and I saw it three times. Super cool flick, though."

"No excuse to skimp on the T & A," Gil said. "It was the '80s! Then there's his Fulci-inspired *Satan Save Me!* and *Maximum Occult.* Gratuitous skin galore."

I said, "Wait, Stanley Fischer. I forgot he's German."

"He was then," Gil said. "English father, by the way. Stan and his companion, Sandahl Urban, live in Western New York, near Syracuse. Fischer is familiar with the Barnhouses. Roger and Ken are musicians'-musicians. Nice way of saying they've done coke with everybody. I told him about my problem and he's eager to meet you. He decided to combine my to-do with a local media conference going on downtown as we speak. His next panel isn't until 9 P.M. Can't say he'll be any help, but the man's a hoot." He removed his apron and led us into the house.

There were a hell of a lot more people inside, blobbing and unblobbing to blob again as one does at these sorts of engagements. Polo shirts and leisure suits aplenty; summer dresses and sandals for the ladies. Youngs and olds mixed freely, united in their kinship as Hollyweirdos. I got an earful as we passed through the kitchen into the living room.

—*killed a man. We were camping in the Adirondacks. Clocked him in the head with a stick.*

No fucking way. Why?

He was rude.

Oh.

Up a flight of stairs and down a hall.

THE WIND BEGAN TO HOWL

—there were like, what? Three? Four naked bitches in the coffin with him?

Three. And his wife walked in and lost her shit. He ran after her in full makeup, screaming, Baby it's okay! They're European!—

—even if we fuck, I won't reveal my source.

—Governor Mario Cuomo Memorial Bridge, my ass. We're going to keep calling it the Tappan Zee Bridge. See me in ten years on that one.

Another flight of stairs, another hall.

—Dude says, she's totally hot out of the corner of your eye—

—we were hanging in Vile's basement smoking dope. Kid says let's check out the locked trunk in mom and dad's room. Vile pops the lock. Loads of VCR tapes of bestiality. Everyone is horrified—

—A guy strolls into camp, covered in blood and carrying his severed arm. Calmly details wildcat attack and asks for help—

The third flight was short and steep and ended in Gil's stuffy attic office. Its peak roof slanted so I had to stand in the center or duck. Here were his computer and bulky graphics processing equipment. A convoluted slate flow chart hung on the door. Pink Floyd, Conan the Barbarian, and Star Wars posters were tacked up, likely having migrated from Gil's childhood bedroom. A man and a woman reposed upon a chaise lounge under a pall of blue-lit dope smog.

Gil introduced the eminent pulp director, Stanley Fischer and Fischer's Austrian expat bodybuilder girlfriend of two decades, Sandahl Urban. He was in his early sixties and grizzled as a vagrant who needed to skip back to the mission for a 5 P.M. shave. Chicken legs, chicken arms, potbellied. Wiry from amphetamines and high-rep kettle bells. She clocked in a few years younger; wiry and craggy with a meanness in her squint, the set of her jaw. Meanness is a plus for competition. Both wore tank tops and gym shorts. He, half-laced combat boots; she, brand spanking new high-top sneakers. His tattoos were distinctively jailhouse; hers were crisper, expensive.

"Love your movies, man," Lionel said to Fischer. "*Synthetic Reflex* scared me even more than *The Terminator*. Buzzsaws and drill bits are visceral."

"*The Terminator* was corporatized crap," the haggard director said with zero accent, except the nonspecific type that pegs one as vaguely European or an expat American. "Tickles me pink Harlan Ellison finally got paid by those Hollywood bloodsuckers." He winked at Gil.

Urban grabbed my hand and squeezed with bone-crushing power. I tried not to wince as my arthritis-weakened joints protested, and in that instant regretted mocking Clupach's fish-grip. I doubted she was a man hater. Probably an everyone hater. She recognized me as a powerlifter, which is to say a cat recognizing a dog. They either coexist or strive to murder one another.

Fischer rose to squint at me.

"Wide load, aren't you? Gil says you own a dog. I never owned a dog. Not even as a child. My father hated animals, especially dogs. Considered them carriers of filth and disease. Much like children in that regard. Bragged he smashed them with his car whenever possible. Doubtful—we drove past curs and he kept steady on. Talked a game, my dad. Personally, I'm indifferent. A German Shepherd bit my left testicle." He grabbed his crotch to demonstrate. "Seized hold tight as you please. Popped it."

"Dummy was climbing a fence to escape the cops," Urban said. Her accent was thicker. "Dog could not be evaded."

"Furry bastard had springs in its legs. Yanked me off that fence, too. Eh, you smile? I assure you, it was no joke to me."

"Sorry, I was visualizing the scene," I said.

"But you're a fan of doggos. Score one for the noble curs, right?"

"Score one for Darwinism, at least." I'd already decided we couldn't be friends.

"Lemme tell you about the dogs of Chernobyl," he said.

"Another time, perhaps."

"Okay. Or the Fukushima Reactor pigs—"

"No thanks," I said.

"Your sympathy extends to the porcine demographic? Astonishing!"

Gil glanced over his shoulder.

"Hey, kids! Anybody want to see a rough cut of *The Wind Began to Howl?*"

"Do I? Do I?" Lionel waved his lighter.

CHAPTER SEVEN
(The 10ᵗʰ Configuration)

We made ourselves comfortable in the stifling haze of the attic.

"The concept crystallized after I listened to 'Boötes & 68.' Gil fiddled with the settings. "The whole Barnhouse catalogue is an inspiration, but that song sank its hooks in. Haunted me. Then I wrote a script. Trashed it and wrote another…"

"Yeah, yeah, 'Boötes & 68' landed while I was in prison," Fischer said. "Deserved a wide release, which the Powers That Be denied. It's an earworm, okay. 'Don't Forget the Gravy' should be the convict's anthem, nonetheless. Brings a tear to my eye."

The oversized monitor resolved to faux Latin placemark credits. Unsettling orchestral music swelled; a cosmic void, pulsating with pinks and violets, resolved to the steady shot of a field of dry grass. Blood dripped from stems. The shadow of a carrion bird wheeled on high. Flies crawled. The music ceased and only ambient sounds remained—whispering grass, buzzing flies, distant bird calls. Dark shapes slithered along the ground. Rustling, crunching, as of some large animal dragging itself forward. The bird calls rose in agitation.

Offscreen, an electronically modulated voice said, "There's always something worse."

A dirty, bloody, feminine hand, reached up and covered the lens. Black. Wind among the grass; twigs snapping. The soft orchestral melody swelled, and beneath it, a klaxon. As the klaxon grew louder and more strident, it morphed into a woman shrieking.

"Shut it off," Urban said. "I can't bear any more of this." She turned her head and smacked Fischer's arm and muttered I didn't know what.

The onscreen cries pitched beyond human threshold. A rabbit in a snare. It's difficult to describe the primordial agony that transmitted itself into the witnesses gathered there. Some demonic combination of subliminal psychedelic imagery and infrasound. Lionel's expression had gone flat.

"Yeah, okay," Fischer said. "Kill it, please. Yes, Gil, kill it."

Gil killed it. Too late. Urban puked into a wastebasket. I empathized, although the nausea soon dissipated.

"That's the Barnhouse technique." Fischer wiped his brow. "Not merely a sample...You adapted their entire method. Crazy motherfucker."

THE WIND BEGAN TO HOWL

"No, no, I *extrapolated* their method. Can't wholly recreate the effect. The full sample occurs near the midway point of the film. We, the sound engineer and I, applied an infrasound effect throughout. Barnhouse lite." Gil watched Urban pull her head out of the bucket. His expression was less sympathetic and more scientifically curious. "May need to dial it back, huh?"

I said, "What's the plot? The high concept pitch. No pun intended."

"To explain the plot, I must preface it with an explanation. The theme of *The Colossal Nothing* is a major influence. The album runs over an hour. The final eleven minutes are pure infrasound bubbling at the limits of perception. It's a hidden track called 'The Void Manifests.' I combined their cosmic nihilism—an emptiness of such mind-boggling vastness, it crowds aside rational thought—with earthly materialism."

"Tits and violence," Lionel said. "That's the pitch."

"Good pitch," I said.

"Yeah," Gil said. "Full frontal male nudity, too. Gets a wee scatological. As for a plot, there's a witch coven dating back to druidic circles of the Dark Ages. These ladies are very gnarly advocates of ritual sacrifice, orgies, and demon summoning. The coven is under surveillance by a government think-tank interested in harnessing sorcery to enhance space exploration and an imminent first-contact situation with an extra-terrestrial intelligence. The coven is captured and subjected to heinous experiments and coercive torture. Experiments go awry in the worst ways imaginable. Essentially everybody dies. Some more horribly than others. Main characters are the Vice President and a younger initiate of the coven. Star-crossed lovers, man."

"You went too far, Gil. I'm sorry, baby." Fischer rubbed Urban's back.

Gil said, "I had a nosebleed listening to *The Colossal Nothing* with high-fidelity ear phones. This is a sort of a Lynchian vibe—*Lost Highway* and the *Twin Peaks* revival. Noe's injection of low-frequency sound into *Irreversible* caused walkouts…"

I hated and feared infrasound for two reasons. One: because that's the noise I heard when I entered a berserker rage. Crackling radiation at the core of a boiling sun. Then the crackling built louder and louder until it rivaled an air raid klaxon. Two: I'd been on the receiving end of Cold War-era sonic weaponry on a case prior to this chapter of my ongoing saga. Experimental, horrible. Long story. Suffice to say, it exacerbated my brain trauma and I wasn't a fan. Gil's movie was going to take a few people to very uncomfortable places if it ever got released.

He said, "Wild to think I'm honing in on their method. Ken mentioned that black science was the foundation of their theory of music, their theory of what music is capable of doing on a large scale. Like mixing culling songs and prayer chants with mind control via hypnotic suggestion and infrasound.

Referenced Tesla and killing frequencies. Had a few ideas regarding the CIA and its experiments. He was stoned, but his words gave me goosebumps."

"I was an asset for the CIA." Urban sounded hoarse, and perhaps embarrassed to have shown mortal frailty in front of three macho dudes and a nerd.

"You *wanted* to be an asset," Fischer said.

I wondered how often she *wanted* to kick his ass.

"No, I wanted to officially join the CIA. Anybody can be an asset. Remember when we filmed in Afghanistan and spent the night at gunpoint in that village…?"

Fischer said, "Rocky swore on his life we weren't spies!"

"He was wrong."

"What the hell are you saying?" The director appeared genuinely surprised.

"Rocky was our guide," she said to me. "We were traveling for other reasons. Stan agreed to help an independent filmmaker with a documentary that wasn't ever released. Anyhow, Stan had a camera and shot footage. I was auditioning for the Company. Counting fighters, taking note of supplies and infrastructure."

"Oh my god," Fischer said. "We could've been murdered!" He smiled wryly and pinched her cheek. "Oh, you madwoman. This is why I love you so."

She slapped his hand and said, "This may interest you, Mr. Coleridge: the warlord confiscated what he pleased of our personal effects. Batteries, chemical handwarmers, candy, and DVDs. He adored Western musicians. John Denver, Willie Nelson, Primus, and…The Barnhouse Effect. Everything changed the moment after he ransacked our bags and saw a limited edition of *The Colossal Nothing.*"

"Cut us loose," Fischer said. "Fed us dinner, and lectured us on music theory until the cock crowed."

"Well, it's a small world after all," I said with less sarcasm than the exchange warranted. "I'm glad you escaped. I hope Langley garnered actionable intel."

"We tell you this story for a reason. The album is cursed, right honey?"

"The brothers are cursed, so naturally they made a cursed record," Urban said.

"The album seems to have been good luck in your case," I said.

"Not in a broader sense."

"Okay. I'll bite."

"Broader!" Urban gesticulated. "Sadly, those two are innocents in a world of vile darkness. Neither of them comprehends what they've wrought nor how evil men might make use of their art. Same to you, Gil! Following in their tracks with this prideful foolishness. Your nose "bled" listening to *The Colossal Nothing*, and what lesson do you take? You create a film incorporating the worst, insidious elements!"

I waited a beat.

"So, we're not discussing a specific evil perpetrated by the Barnhouses. Vague, amorphous evil?"

THE WIND BEGAN TO HOWL

"Theoretical evil," Lionel said.

Gil shook his head with an exasperated grimace.

"C'mon! The album isn't cursed. Some critic invented that rumor. As they used to say when you play rock songs backwards, Satan speaks. The Barnhouses aren't cursed, either. Just really, really unfortunate."

Urban said, "I've peered into their souls. I've read their palms. Cursed!"

"There's a girlfriend," I said. "She might know more."

"Krystal Niven," Fischer said. "Nice. You should definitely speak to her."

Urban gave him the look of death.

"Oh yeah, Stan. Nice? You think she's got nice tits. The girl is very odd. She's been in trouble. Can't trust gold diggers."

"Krystal's been through the wars and seen everything." Red-eyed and bleary, Fischer reached over and clasped my arm in a brotherly gesture. "I listen to my guts and my guts say the Barnhouses have secluded themselves. Artists must seek the solace of isolation from time to time. Many believe they've retired. An erroneous assumption. *The Colossal Nothing* might not be the end. I wager they're busy recording a true epic. The epic to surpass everything. A magnum opus!"

"Where?" I perked up.

"At a secret studio called Wails and Moans."

"Secret in what way?"

"In the sense that they refused to divulge its location. Harms owns it. They were so precious in regard to cutting *The Colossal Nothing,* including their process."

"Less helpful than I'd hoped."

"Take heart, sir. Roger and Ken occasionally rent a cabin in the boondocks." He gestured vaguely. "South side of Harpy Peak in the Catskills. Sandy and I have camped with them there. Comfortable, intimate. Ken mentioned he'd preferred it to bunking at the studio. I inferred this meant it was in the region. Of course, I didn't press. Ken is volatile. The quiet types, yeah? Underestimate them at your peril."

"Any chance you might share the address?" I said.

A light animated Fischer's expression.

"Consider a proposition—I'll speak with the realtor and see if he'll let the place. You and your manservant can join us for a few days. We have a panel at the convention tomorrow and other engagements early in the coming week. Wednesday, perhaps? Headquarter at the cabin while you check the surrounding area. If the brothers are around, someone will remember."

"Not a terrible idea," Lionel said.

Fischer said, "There's an item at the cabin that may pique your curiosity. An artifact of sorts."

"Sold," Lionel said.

I grunted noncommittally. It was exactly how I felt.

CHAPTER EIGHT
(Polanski & Cher Attack)

No matter how sneaky, no matter how determined to vanish into the ether, you can't hide forever. Cops, bounty hunters, and private detectives command virtually unlimited resources to comb through known associates, childhood friends, and exes. Any breadcrumb you've dropped will be vacuumed sooner or later. The fishing cabin you mentioned to a bartender back when? We know. An alias based on some BBB handle from the 90s? Cover blown. Credit card user? Blinking arrow overhead. Pay in cash? Some nosy clerk, somewhere, will recognize your beady-eyed mug. You'll be found. That ticking you hear is the countdown clock.

Monday, I spent the morning on the phone delivering bad news about cheating spouses, photographic evidence of insurance claim cheats, one stalker, and a partridge in a pear tree. Typical morning in the life of Coleridge Investigations. Ted struck out searching for info regarding the studio, Wails and Moans.

Red McLaren and I did lunch at Da Vinci Deli in East Kingston. He'd counseled my agency for a while and understood exactly how it was with me. 'Speak no evil, hear no evil, et cetera,' was a stock line of his. Also, "Hypothetically speaking…" Fortunately for him, the majority of our interactions consisted of ascertaining I'd properly obeyed bureaucratic protocols such as filing requisite government forms in triplicate. Incidentally, he wrote a mean-as-hell cease and desist letter. Reviewing Barnhouses' three-page contract over a second cup of black coffee, he concluded it was standard stuff. This dovetailed with my own admittedly untutored assessment.

His only comment: "Clupach, Ransom, and Friend. Sounds shady as hell. A C-note says they're mobbed up. Uh, nothing personal."

Walking to my truck, I received a text from the day shift guy keeping tabs on Krystal Niven. He lurked across the street with an eagle-eye view. A suspicious couple had entered the complex parking lot. I immediately called him to get the play-by-play on speaker. Short man, brown jacket; tall woman in a gray pantsuit, resembled Cher in her vampy days. Cher watched as her partner casually popped the lock on Niven's Kia and climbed inside. Low traffic and the couple were smooth. Nobody paid them any attention.

I was already behind the wheel, speeding toward the unfolding incident. As I weaved through traffic, my stakeout guy blandly related that the brown jacket dude finished tossing the car...now the pair were headed inside Niven's unit. Should he take action? No, I was three minutes out, sit tight.

Ninety seconds, actually. I zoomed into the Hudson Villa South Lot and parked across two empty guest spaces. The blocks contained four units apiece: drab, weathered beige. Niven lived on the second floor, above an elderly woman and her cats. According to Ted's info, the remaining units were unoccupied. Normally, I would've maintained distance and let the scenario reach its natural conclusion. However, I'm a creature of instinct and instinct warned me I'd regret not intervening on Krystal Niven's behalf. .38 snub on my ankle, jawbone knife in my pocket, I proceeded, bulldozer mode activated. The foyer entrance wasn't secured. And people wondered why crime flourishes in Kingston.

I hit the stairs at a jog. The door to apartment 4C was ajar. Typical layout for a midrange two-bedroom. Leather couch, bookshelves, reproduction Van Goghs, a beanbag chair, and the like. TV hanging on the wall was tuned to a soap. Scents of lavender and citrus air freshener. I knew the kitchen would be neat as a pin and the bedroom and bathroom messy and a pigsty respectively. The man in the brown jacket nudged magazines lying on the coffee table. He turned quickly when I strolled in. Short and as muscular as a wrestler. Slick, out-of-fashion haircut. Sharp features and stubble. His appearance put me in mind of '60s, and '70s detective flicks emulating shows from the '40s and '50s. I dubbed him Polanski. Partly because a young Polanski was the impression I got, and second, I'd longed to punch the director in the mouth since my teens. Cher bopped out of the bedroom. Yep, she was as advertised, except lankier. She carried a laptop computer under her arm.

"Hello, handsome," Polanski said. So, we established right off the bat he was a liar. He didn't reach for a weapon, which was good. Instead, he relaxed into a semi-crouch, which *wasn't* so good.

"I'm here to take Krissy to the purity ball." I angled toward him, smiling an idiotic smile. "She ready?"

Cher eschewed pleasantries. She flung the laptop at me, hopped over the couch, and whipped a telescoping military grade baton upward from her hip. I raised my left arm reflexively. Stung like a dog bite. The follow-up slapped my ribs, and that hurt too, but I was moving, set to collide with her partner. Today I'd worn a T-shirt, jeans, and steel toe boots. All offense, no defense.

I feinted low and grabbed Polanski's throat, which surprised and alarmed him. Plan was to ram the little guy through one those plaster walls. He pivoted, broke my grip on the thumb side with an edge-of-the-hand chop, and neatly sidestepped as I stumbled past. I wheeled and caught a double-jab to the eye. Not much on them; enough to discombobulate me, to set me on my heels.

Polanski proved slippery as a serpent, landing crisp shots over, under, and around my guard while evading my sluggish retaliatory swipes. I didn't recognize the combat style; his fluid stance and selection of elbow, palm, and raking strikes suggested an East Indian tradition. Working in expert tandem, Cher stayed at mid-range to whack my arms as I formed a turtle shell.

Whap! A left hook to my jaw. *Thwap!* An uppercut to my chin.

Snow filled my tunnel vision. The TV blared.

—after these messages—

Thud! Thwok! Baton to the nose and again to the wrist. A blizzard of sensation, then numbness lit by jagged streaks of fire. Misery upon misery. Multiplicities of misery.

—Palm Olive dish soap is the leader—

Thump! A flying knee to the sternum. My breath wooshed out. Lung-charring fire rushed in.

—double your pleasure with the extralong flavor—

The savage animal preserve of my deep consciousness shrieked and thundered. The beast yearned to usurp control in the worst way, yearned to summon the hideous red light of Jupiter's eye, to unholster my ankle revolver and commence blasting. I stifled that impulse and waded forward, blocking what I could, eating the rest. A new battle plan failed to coalesce; my sole desire was to stop the snap-kicks, punches, and baton wallops. An insidious leaden exhaustion weighted my limbs. Gravity doubled. Anybody who's swum too far, too fast, or fought in a ring and received a beating knows whereof I speak.

Thank God I spotted a table out of my flickering peripheral vision, else the beating might've gone on forever. I abandoned my hodgepodge boxing and Krav Maga repertoire and went full bore Saturday night WWF. I bench four hundred pounds for reps; the table hefted, light as balsa wood. Snatched it and swung broadside at my tormentors, a hoplite winging his aspis with dire intent.

Cher danced away clean.

Clobbered Polanski, though.

Luckily for him, the cheap furniture shattered on impact.

He staggered, windmilling through the door into the hall.

Cher pitched her baton and it caromed off my skull.

Lots of pretty lights whirled in blinding constellations. The fog of blindness, of sleep…

I yanked the door shut and collapsed onto the couch. Fumbled the pistol loose, tried to steady my trembling arm. My fighting spirit had evaporated; anybody sticking his or her snout into this room would find themselves ventilated. Blood streamed into my eyes. Blood poured down my throat from my

THE WIND BEGAN TO HOWL

smashed nose. Sucking a red-hot lungful of oxygen, I wadded a tablecloth and pressed it to the gash under my hairline. Hunched there like a gory, battered cave bear after he's driven off the hounds. I sulked, licked the blood oozing from my skinned knuckles.

Finally registered my phone buzzing. Reliable Lowlife texted, mildly curious to know if everything was okay. Hunky-dory, I assured him. Had he seen which direction the couple fled? After a hesitation, he said they must be inside the building. Nobody had emerged since I charged in a couple of minutes ago. By the way, sirens were swiftly approaching. The Cat Lady in 1C must've alerted Five-Oh.

French doors squeaked open in the hall. A woman peeked out of the closet. She weighed the wreckage of her living room, then stared at me.

"You're alive," she said. "They were really kicking your ass."

"They really were," I said.

CHAPTER NINE
(Krystal Blue Persuasion)

A squad of Kingston's finest rolled up, interviewed us, photographed the scene, and were intensely dissatisfied. Krystal Niven vouched for me, which helped. I demoed my PI license, which *didn't* impress. We told them exactly what was required and not an iota more. For her part, Krystal ducked into the closet when she heard the door getting jimmied. I explained my presence as a routine visit inspired by providence. The boys in blue poked around downstairs; didn't find any evidence of a break-in. Possibly Cher and Polanski fled through the security door, although that would've triggered an alarm. The cops remained discontent. Nonetheless, they had papers to shuffle and doughnuts to eat. One of them confiscated the baton and they were gone.

Krystal wrapped a bag of ice in a towel and traded it for her tablecloth. Forty-three, according to her files. Blonde, pale, light makeup. Wore a hoodie and sweats. Charm bracelet, no ring. Freshly done red nails. Sandals. Cool as the ice numbing my scalp. What I knew—lifelong New Yorker; New Paltz grad; divorced; childless; rap sheet for minor possession and disorderly conduct. Assault and battery charge dropped for punching her ex, an alleged violent drunk. Sounded A-okay to me.

She skeptically examined my card, my bloody thumbprint.

"Isaiah Coleridge. Detective. Your aura is wrong. For some reason, I figured you were lying to the cops."

"Only when necessary."

"Well, detective. Rye or bourbon?"

"Rye."

She fetched a bottle of Old Forester and poured two glasses.

"Not to tell you your business or anything, but a doctor might want to check you for a concussion."

"Nothing a fistful of Vicodin won't remedy." My nose had already swollen. Deep, abiding pain set in.

She disappeared and returned with a few extra-strength aspirin.

I swallowed them with the whiskey, counting loose teeth.

"Here's the deal. I need to serve papers on Roger and Ken. A music contract. Our mutual acquaintance, Tod Lyra, claims you accept, er, correspondence on their behalf. I had someone clocking your apartment."

"There are more guys blundering around the bushes?" Her gaze turned to the window.

"Good thing, huh?

"Okay. I don't have any way to reach Roger or Ken. They get ahold of me on their own terms."

"Huh, I keep hearing that line. You happen to know Cher and Polanski?"

"Who?"

"The intruders."

"Yeah," she said. "And no. Haven't been introduced, but I've seen those fuckers in the hedgerow before. NSA, DoD, CIA, pick one. Roger and Ken got mixed up with that crowd after leaving the Army." She sighed. "I love Rog. I love Ken-Ken. I don't love the heat." She polished off her drink. Her hands shook. "My hunch? Cordell Harms is responsible. He's—"

"The Barnhouses' producer."

"Former producer," she said. "He glommed on to them when they were weak, directionless youngsters. The Moonies and other cults recruited from bus depots and train stations, trying to snag runaways and kids newly discharged from the military. New motherfucker, same cult methodology. Roger and Ken distanced themselves once *The Colossal Nothing* was finished. They planned to produce any future albums themselves, planned to go full indie. Or quit the industry altogether and go on adventures. Mountain climbing in Nepal, spelunking, blue hole diving…

"Parasites like Harms are relentless, though. It's his style. He's called me to finagle the guys' location several times. Charm offensive, then more ominous.

'I'm worried, Krystal. The lads are emotionally fragile. All great artists are!' and so on. Now this." She gestured at the wreckage.

"Harms worked for the State Department," I said. "You figure he has access to former agents to run his errands."

"Bingo. Intelligence Bureau in the '80s. I didn't realize how far back he and the guys went or that he'd played ball for Uncle Sam until he casually mentioned it one night. This was, oh, almost a decade ago. To me he was simply Cordell moneybags. We were 'shrooming our asses off at his apartment in the city—"

"Who's we?"

"The boys and Stan Fischer—he's a director. Does science fiction flicks and supernatural horror."

"We've met. Fischer dropped your name."

"Yeah? We were tripping. Harms broke out a slide projector and showed a few pics of his glory days in Central America. I mean, I doubt it was top-secret-now-I-gotta-kill-you information. Unsettling. That light in his eyes, reliving bad shit he did. Bonus detail—your so-called Polanski and Cher dropped by for a minute. Harms had a whisper-conference at the door. He didn't say who they were. I've since filled in the dots. Fellow intelligence ops. Henchmen."

Fischer and Urban's conversation came to mind. Though initially dismissing them as cranks, I had the burgeoning sense this small crowd of misfit musicians, filmmakers, and gadflies was actually embroiled in wicked shenanigans. This type of dynamic was complicated in that people weren't necessarily concealing information; often, they simply didn't know what they actually knew.

I held out my empty glass. She poured three fingers worth.

"Why bust in here?" A rhetorical question. Polanski and Cher could've had numerous motives.

"Same reason *you* darkened my doorstep. Shitbirds were hunting for clues…As if. Monday is arm day. Noon to 2 P.M. It's only a ten-minute walk. So, I walk. Except today I felt blah. Stayed in to watch TV, catch up on my email…"

"Your visitors expected an empty apartment," I said. "The woman had what I presume is your computer…"

"Would've made more sense to mug me for my phone. There're spread sheets, tax returns, and junk on the laptop. Glorified word processor."

"It would be nice to corner Harms for a chat. He's a difficult man to get on the phone."

"By design," she said. "Lives out of a suitcase when he wants to lower his profile. He reappears in a puff of black smoke."

"The million-dollar question—why did your buddies pull a vanishing act?"

"Besides the fact they're kooks? Told you, they're in hiding. Same as it ever was—the shape of the stars, coded messages on the side of a cereal box gets their wind up and they vanish into the wild blue yonder. Time passes and they bop back into my life as if nothing happened. It's a persistent shitty pattern."

Sorrow etched her face and I was tempted to hug her. Instead, I kept pressing.

"Or, could it be they're working on new music? Fischer thinks so. Filled me in on the Catskill getaway. Maybe two things can be true. Fischer's theory intrigues me, nonetheless. He predicts we'll find your boys bunkered down in a top-secret studio making sweet music."

"Wouldn't put a lot of stock in his 'theory.' Fucker is certifiable."

I couldn't argue against her statement after my afternoon with the man. Even so, a lead was a lead.

"Fischer not your tempo? My impression is he's enamored of you."

"Didn't say I dislike him. I said he's certifiable."

"And a fucker."

"He's a Hollywood hack, his bullshit protestations to the contrary. He'd sell his soul to pilot a summer blockbuster."

"What of the studio? Does it exist?"

"Yeah, Wails and Moans exists." She crossed her arms. "Been around since the 1970s, from what I gather. Harms bought it and takes special acts to record. But, you said the magic word: it's secret, y'know? I haven't actually seen it and they didn't give any hints. Boys Club."

"Has to be within driving range of the cabin." When she didn't answer, I said, "Anywhere you can go while I sort this out? Might be wise to lie low, like your homies."

She smiled a bright, cynical smile.

"Oh, going to get this sorted? Do tell."

"Geez, lady. Not by my lonesome. I have friends. Associates. Minions."

Krystal looked at the blood plinking onto my boots.

"God, the carpet is ruined. Asshole landlord will turn loose of my deposit when hell freezes."

"I'll talk to him. This should be a secure building. Pure negligence."

"You absolutely would, huh?"

"I absolutely will."

Krystal packed a bag and I checked her into a Rosendale motel. I put my guy on the place as a watchdog and directed him to call the cops if any bogeys appeared. By then, I was feeling like a lump of tenderized round steak.

A nurse of my acquaintance met me in her garage where she treated all her illicit clients. Checked for internal injuries and stitched the worst of my lacerations. My nose was broken, but would heal without interference. She didn't bother insisting on a hospital visit for X-rays, knowing well my position on the US medical system—I only visited the hospital when dragged. I crossed her palm with several bills and she sent me on my way with a baggie of generic painkillers and a fare-thee-well. I went home to face the music with Meg.

Lionel was mowing the yard with a push mower, shirtless. Devlin ran past him and uttered a shrill cry. Lionel answered with a death gurgle.

I exited the truck. Lionel stared at my battered face, then laughed so hard he rolled on the grass.

"Hail, brother," he said upon recovering. "It's like I'm gazing into a freakin' mirror."

Devlin showed a smidgeon more empathy.

"Isaiah, what happened?"

"Got into a fight," I said.

"You lost!" the boy said in awe and horror as his lower lip trembled.

Meg greeted us inside, expression carefully neutral. She leaned into me and sniffed my neck and shredded shirt.

"Interesting fragrance. Chanel?"

"Baby, I can explain."

"Lionel," she said. "Would you mind taking Devlin to Cherry's for ice cream? He's been on my case all week for a sundae. There's cash in my purse in the kitchen."

I didn't hear what Lionel said because Meg grabbed my shirt sleeve, marched me into the bedroom, and had her way with me. None too gentle, either.

Later, flat on my back and half-alive, I said, "My pain and suffering does it for you, eh? Or handsome shirtless guys flaunting themselves in the yard?"

She smiled and spread her thumb and index finger slightly.

"You're perfect." My tears leaked. Happiness, or pain. Both.

Meg and Devlin were glued to a program chronicling humankind's space exploration. These were the last hours of twilight glory prior to the resumption of school. I sat on the porch with Lionel and Minerva in the gathering dark. I sipped a glass of lemonade splashed with vodka. He smoked a cigarette and clutched a beer while I narrated the afternoon's excitement concluding with Krystal's belief that mystery man Cordell Harms was the mastermind.

"You left a message for Harms. Hope that doesn't come back to bite us."

"Nothing specific." Worried, I altered course. "Let's focus on what we can control. Such as payback for me getting so thoroughly jumped." My lumpen cheek radiated heat. Resentment kindled in my heart.

"Lucky your jaw doesn't need to be wired shut. Five years ago, you would've easily prevailed."

"Hey! It was a legitimate draw against two skilled foes."

"How many draws on your score card *before* today?"

I didn't give him the satisfaction of a riposte.

"Rang Fischer to accept his offer to visit the cabin. Gil's coming."

"Great, another supervisor. Lawyers are cheap bastards. Betcha that Blues Clues, Random, and Fuckface are sending him to eyewitness report where the money is going."

"Let's bring Niven with us too."

"For what good reason?"

"Safer under our tender care. Plus, to keep an eye on her in case she knows more. Might slip. Meg asked me to take Minerva. Breaks the dog's heart whenever I leave on an overnighter."

He shook his head.

"Goddamned *Fellowship of the Ring* action going on."

"I envision it as a Hercule Poirot gambit. Gather the suspects under one roof and wait."

"Fun."

"All of this is too pat—the contract that needs to be signed at all costs, Fischer and Urban happening to roll into town, the Bobbsey Twins busting a move on our damsel in distress…"

"Thus, the Agatha Christie retreat," he said. "Do recall, the last two remote cabins we've visited were bad news." He referenced nasty cases in the not-so-distant past.

I said, "Gil and his circle may or may not be holding out, but I kinda hope they are, amigo."

"Aw, the mean old you has returned."

"Rattle my cage, the door gets unlocked." I spat, searching my memories for a time when my mouth wasn't full of blood.

Whiro, Māori god of evil, shouted at me from a cave in a mountain. He wore a suit and reared as tall as a giant. Diminutive clones of himself descended the bone-strewn slope, claws stretched toward me. We were longtime frenemies in these nightmares. I rolled over. My phone glowed on the bedside table.

Bruce Clupach, Esq. had texted:
Don't despair, my friend
Don't B discouraged
U will receive a bonus
We're counting on U

Obviously, I texted him back. The message bounced.

PART II
LEE VAN CLEEF

CHAPTER TEN
(Searchers in Darkness)

I loaded the usual supplies for the trip north—toothbrush, socks, clean underwear, some guns. A coat of body armor. Treats for Minerva and a worn-out paperback of *Ghost Story* by Peter Straub. Meg loaned me her Caravan after extracting my solemn oath to not wreck it or get it shot full of holes. I may have crossed my fingers behind my back as I kissed her goodbye. Fischer, Urban, and Gil met us in Kingston in the afternoon. They'd rented an SUV. Gil abandoned his homies and hopped into the backseat of the Caravan with Lionel and Krystal. Krystal had hemmed and hawed in regard to coming along for the ride. I convinced her she'd be safer with me than on her own. Her eyes narrowed when Lionel introduced himself. He was still bashed all to hell, but she apparently gave nary a damn. Oh, boy, here we go again is what I thought. I managed to keep my mouth shut.

Krystal did say something odd.

"Dreamt of Ken and Roger again. Eighth night in a row." She laughed a brittle, self-conscious laugh. "We practiced sending telepathic messages. Roger was convinced the brain is a transceiver. Simply requires practice."

Minerva rode shotgun.

Gil blanched at the sight of mangled me. "Oh, man. Oh, man! Are you okay to drive?"

"Downed a fistful of pills at breakfast," I said. "Feeling great, and expecting to feel even better!" His expression was worth the pain of keeping a straight face.

Hot, bright weather persisted. I followed Route Twenty-eight past Phoenicia. Traffic would thicken as Labor Day approached. Our destination represented a winter attraction and summer vacationers gravitated toward beaten paths. A minor break; I wasn't in a mood to contend with jocular crowds. Calculating by the map, it would be a circuitous hour and forty-minute drive, plus or minus, to reach the vicinity of the cabin, dubbed Manley Ridge.

My backseat passengers chatted happily, passing a joint. Gil sat in the middle and his expression gradually dulled into pleading, then apathy. I felt guilty whenever I checked the rearview mirror.

"Married for nine years," Krystal said. "Three great, three bad, three dragging a body through the woods. Got divorced, embarked on a six-month drunk and was hitchhiking on the interstate when Roger and Ken stopped in their van. Middle of the night en route to a gig. I became their Groupie of One." This immediately spiraled into a startlingly frank and graphic discussion of her and Lionel's romantic misadventures, one or two I hadn't heard before. My compadre was a man of hidden depths and locked compartments. I turned up the radio. Alas, they yelled over a Hall and Oates Super Eighties Rock Block.

We stopped at a general store to top off the tanks and grab chips and jerky. Lionel and Krystal carried on in line.

"Booze is truth serum." She eyed his purchases. "I may have some probing questions."

"See you next time." The cashier pushed beer and smokes across the counter without making eye contact.

"The Oracle speaks," Lionel said.

Meanwhile, Gil raced back to the pumps to escape with Fischer and Urban, who zoomed away, leaving him adrift in a cloud of dust. Gil glumly settled for a window seat.

I stepped on the gas to catch the SUV.

Lionel said, "I'm addicted to internet videos of karmic justice. My whole jam, lately."

"Karmic justice?" Krystal said.

"Bullies screwing with the wrong victim is always entertaining."

"Oh, road ragers getting punched out! Victims

beating down muggers! Love it. They're sooo relaxing. You can pour out a glass of red and luxuriate."

"My second-favorite genre has to be pirates meeting their deserved fates."

"Pirates?" she said. "Yo-ho-ho and a bottle of rum? I thought they went the way of the dodo."

Lionel popped the top of his beer.

"More or less, except instead of the 17th Century Caribbean, we're talking off the coast of Somalia and places like that. There's a video series of mercs aboard merchant vessels shooting the living shit out of yahoos in speedboats. I'm no fan of mercenaries, nonetheless, when push comes to shove, I'm less sanguine about anarchy on the high seas."

"Do the mercenaries really shoot them?" she said. "It's on video?"

"The *nice* guys fire warning shots when the pirates are hundreds of yards out. *Nice* guys skip bullets off the water and give the bogeys a chance to do right and turn around. Some of those mercs aren't nice— bona fide mofos. The hardcore dudes and their homies hide under deck tarps and wait until the ragamuffin motherfuckers pull alongside and try to scale the hull. The mercs pop up and give them what for, full auto in the face."

"I dunno," she said. "Kinda excessive, isn't it? Sounds excessive."

"Don't know about excessive. Brutal, yeah. One merc performed a monologue to explain his

THE WIND BEGAN TO HOWL

philosophy. *See, as long as a dude stays onshore, he's a poor economically depressed soul. The second he clambers into a skiff with an AK and a machete and putts my direction, he's a fucking pirate. I shoot pirates.* I can see his point of view."

Krystal said, "Hmm, it might be more nuanced than the opinion of some dirtbag hired to protect highly insured cargo." She changed the subject and soon they'd veered from the supercharged political question of whether it's moral to mow down desperate, hungry people to more esoteric fare.

"Scariest places on earth," she said. "Haunted house, cemetery, or an abandoned mall?"

"Mar-a-Lago and the Playboy Mansion." Lionel crushed his beer can and opened another. "Glitz and glamor on the surface. Tony clientele—"

"Sheiks, actors, celebrities. Famous animals. Bubbles the chimp, the most notable primate to visit either pleasure dome."

"But under the façade of luxury, everything is decrepit and full of specters," Lionel said with boozy conviction. "Lousy food. Lousy people. Bloodstains in the carpets. Vermin of all kinds. To say nothing of the violence. Rapes, murder, international spying…"

"Man, if the cops had blacklight that exposed the aura of gross memories, those joints would echo with psychic screams." The girl was certainly a connoisseur of auras.

"Don't get me started on Las Vegas," Lionel said.

"Many a ghost in Sin City. Those crumbling skeletons at the bottom of holes in the desert. Saw a documentary claiming Bugsy Siegel and Meyer Lansky forged a pact with Satan to get Vegas on the map. Same deal with the coven who created the US interstate. The sources were very credible."

Gil roused.

"As a matter of fact, I read a true account of the satanic origins of—"

"Good grief." Cue my dad glare in the rearview. "Maybe one of you kids should sit up front. Not sure I like this seating arrangement." An idle threat. Minerva grinned, tongue lolling. Gil had already tried to steal her spot and received bared fangs for his troubles. The hound would budge when hell glassed over into a skating rink. I'd made the correct and moral choice, adding her to the expedition. She'd spent the entire night glued to me in bed; muzzle pressed close, her nervous, motherly breaths flooding my nostrils.

Manley Ridge was comprised of a burly log cabin worthy of Grizzly Adams himself, and a handful of rickety outbuildings. Originally a logging or hunting camp, I was fuzzy on which. The property sat right below the tree line of thickly forested mountains near the popular skiing destination of Harpy Peak, which was visible through the canopy on this clear

THE WIND BEGAN TO HOWL

day. Three miles up a winding dirt road from the secondary highway and another fifteen minutes to the nearest town, Helmwood, where we'd paused to acquire the cabin keys from a realtor. Helmwood was the largest of several towns in the radius of Harpy Peak, including Wilder, Smith Town, and Harpy's Glen. My trusty digital map marked the ruins of two resorts dating back to the height of the Borscht Belt era.

Fischer claimed one could drive all the way in to the cabin through early winter. Latter December was iffy. January and February, no way, José. Woodshed and generator shack in the rear—he'd lugged a portable gasoline model in case of emergency. Eastern exposure with a view down into the valley. Then a whole lot more forest—mixed spruce, birch, and maple. Amazingly, the Manley Ridge connected to phone and power lines. Outages lasted days or weeks, however. The rough-hewn log walls were dense. Longhouse style main floor. Kitchen, bathroom, two bedrooms, and a loft. Antlers over the fireplace. Oil landscapes and a hanging swede saw did it for art decor. Throw rugs and heavy wooden furniture. Handmade pinewood bookcases freighted with an eclectic mini-library of clothbound tomes and yellowed paperbacks. Fischer said celebrities occasionally leased the cabin, and an iconoclastic actor had wintered there. The former A-lister refused to join the production of what would be his final, disastrous film. Instead, he dug in and survived a vicious Nor'easter while his ex-wife and ex-talent agent raged in LA. Manley Ridge was built to withstand Mother Nature's worst while the hooch and firewood held out.

Minerva bolted in a frenzy to sniff everything and then piss on it for good measure. My girl, my girl. The rest of us lugged sleeping bags, coolers, and a pile of incidentals, inside. I propped the front door wide to freshen the vague mustiness. One bedroom came with a double; Fischer and Urban called dibs. The second room featured four stout wooden bunks. I selected a lower berth so Minerva could snuggle. Though it appeared sturdy, I didn't relish testing my two-hundred-and-fifty pounds on the kiddie ladder.

We finished digging in at sunset. A brassy haze gradually dimmed and clotted to match my own tapestry of bruises. Every tenderized muscle ached. I'd only joked about the pills earlier. Now I swallowed a couple and got to work on a can of Lionel's bargain beer. Minerva cleaved to my side as full dark stole over the land and a few stars appeared. After her initial hyperactive foray, she'd settled into peevish moodiness unlike her normal self. Her ears flicked and she stared intently into the woods—one direction, then another. Lionel patted her. He retrieved my Mossberg shotgun from the vehicle, checked the load, and stuck it in the corner behind the front door.

"Can't be too safe in black bear country," he said to me in passing.

"Bear country?" Urban dug in her pack and

produced two industrial-sized canisters of bear mace. "Bring them on! I'm prepared!" She twirled them like six-shooters and almost smiled. Almost.

"Most definitely," Lionel said with an approving nod.

"Okay, this is pretty cute," Krystal said, flushed, hands on her hips. "I'm starved. Who's in charge of feeding me?"

Fischer said, "There's a firepit with a grill around the side of the house. Gil, can you handle T-bone steaks as gallantly as you do hamburgers?"

"I'll do or die!"

"Foreshadowing," Lionel said.

I cracked a smile. He didn't return it.

CHAPTER ELEVEN
(The Book of the Void)

Gil assembled a meal of steak and mushrooms, baked potatoes with butter, green beans, and wine and beer to wash it down. Ice cream cake for dessert. We reclined in camp chairs and on firewood logs. Despite my discomfort, my suspicion, and Minerva's squirrelly behavior, it was an admittedly pleasant interlude. Relaxing by a campfire on a summer's evening isn't a bad way to spend an hour or two. Minerva overcame her agitation to patrol the assembly, begging for tidbits. No one minded; Fischer, avowed antagonist of canines everywhere, tossed her a slice of his dinner. Around 11 P.M., the air chilled as it does in subalpine terrain at night, and we retreated inside. I kindled a fire in the hearth to knock off the chill. Gil poured another round, this time the harder stuff. I'd brought scotch; he presented a fine Suntory Hibiki. If nothing else, drink and painkillers reduced my body's protestation to a dull roar.

Urban tinkered with a dusty turntable and put on Billy Joel's *The Stranger*. Everybody was mellow, sacked out on one of the two scaly couches, in the hide-draped wingback chairs, or near the fireplace. Krystal sat close to Lionel on the smaller couch. She wore ripped jeans and pink socks and playfully kicked him whenever he said something hilarious, which was appallingly often. For his part, drunk as hell, he shined with the dull radiance of a diminishing star.

Fischer said, "One must consider the myth of coincidence. The grand theater of existence is subject to probabilities, random variances, chaos and caprice, and yet. A great, hidden hand plucks the strings, orchestrating, controlling."

"AKA producers," Gil said. He'd downed a yeoman's dose of the Suntory whisky and was adorably bellicose.

"I merely ask you to ponder the apparently unconnected strands of happenstance. The Barnhouses crafted a bizarre album; you've taken inspiration and created a tangentially related film. Pieces move. Sandy and I have supped with the brothers and partaken of their psychedelics. Great shit! Half a world away, a tribal warlord absent love for anything American grooves to their funky beats. Wheels turn. Tumblers drop. The brothers are mysteriously gone. This man's poor face..." Fischer indicated me. "Here we gather, perhaps even as forces of darkness gather."

"The planets outside the window gather," I

paraphrased Stevens' famous "Domination of Black" poem. "As the leaves turn in the fire. Snap, crackle, pop."

Fischer ignored the interruption.

"I say unto thee, there's a common undergirding, the grooved tracks which automatons must follow to a scripted tune. A sinister stratagem uncoils, albeit yet to fully manifest."

"Blowin' my mind," Gil said, slurring. An animal squalled in the trees. He sat bolt upright and shuddered. "Anybody heard of the Catskill Devil?"

"What?" Fischer blinked rapidly, doubtless spinning up his mental encyclopedia of crypto-fauna and old wives' tales. He fit the profile of an enthusiast of Bigfoot and suppressed memories of alien abductions.

Lionel wasn't lagging far behind thanks to alcohol-fueled credulity.

"Robert E. Howard spoke of horrors dwelling in the dark crannies of the earth."

"So did Clark Ashton Smith," Gil said.

I struggled to maintain an impassive demeanor; not because Fischer was spouting psychobabble or that my pal was egging him on. I rather believed the crusty director, which meant this whole affair could only end in chaos. My personal saga since relocating to New York had taught me more credulousness in regard to the ineffable. I didn't quite believe in werewolves or ghosts, but moved closer every restless night, every howl in the graveyard hours. Hamlet would've approved.

Krystal theatrically retold my encounter with Cher and Polanski.

"Said it once, I'll say it again." She sloshed the wine in her glass. "Rawest scrap I ever did see, and I was at Woodstock '99."

Fischer grumbled that pillow fights in Cell Block D were rougher and Gil had gone glassy-eyed.

Urban said, "These thugs Krystal describes...I am certain I once saw them at a gathering hosted by Harms. Minions, certainly. Former intelligence operatives. Their posture, the way they move in coordination...specialized training. Military or intelligence." A glass or three of liquor and a few tokes of Acapulco Gold smoothed her rough edges. She'd gotten onboard our game of Clue. "And I have likely confirmed the fact."

"Ha, bitches." Krystal snatched Lionel's cigarette from his fingers and puffed. "Like I said!"

"How do you know this?" Fischer asked his companion.

"My dear," Urban said. "Once again, I've connections at Langley. One of these connections confirmed Harms freelances for several private entities. Zircon Corp; Sword Enterprises; Black Dog, and so on. Coleridge, are you familiar with these organizations? The trio operate globally, yet each maintains a headquarters in New York State."

"To my woe, yes," I said. "Please carry on."

"Gotta see a man about a mule!" Gil gained his feet and lurched for the bathroom.

Urban said, "As a result of his unique professional history, Harms is on friendly terms with numerous government agents. That's the extent of what my source would reveal. I suppose it sounds far-fetched…"

"Not so much," I said.

"Hey, Coleridge, perhaps I shall demonstrate my own magic." Fischer cracked his knuckles and rolled up his sleeves. "Remember, I promised to show you an item of possible interest. I, uh, poked around when I was here recently. Roger and Ken enjoyed journaling. They stashed papers here at the cabin, like squirrels socking away nuts. I saw the hiding spot, one evening two or three years back. The last time we spent a weekend together here. Roger was blotto…"

"Whoa," Krystal said. "Uncool, Stan. You spied on your friends."

"Sorry, I am impulsive. They are haphazard. An unharmonious combination." He was supremely unaffected by his indulgence in copious amounts of beer and evidently possessed the constitution of a Panzer. He pried up a loose floorboard and retrieved an object; cleared a patch of coffee table and met my eye. "I was sorely tempted to bring this home. I *did* peruse it at length."

I said, "If it helps find the guys, I'm eager to see what you have in store."

Fischer laid down a tattered notebook, and spread its pages. The notebook contained a Muybridge-worthy sequence of crude anatomical drawings, geometric figures, and arcane hen scratches in a feverish combination of Tesla, Kaczynski, and H.P. Lovecraft. "This is a diary, journal, what the hell ever you wish to call it. The first entries date to the latter 1990s."

I turned the journal on its side to decipher the handwriting, in vain.

"I've no idea what this is supposed to be."

Krystal said in a grating tone, "Allow me to save you the trouble. This gobbledygook is Roger's theory for accessing higher dimensions of consciousness via a synthesis of mathematical formulae and good ol' black magic: shit, blood, and cum."

"Precisely, young lady!" Fischer had crowded beside me to examine a charcoal sketch of star fields trapped in an obsidian vertical column. "May I?" He eagerly snatched the notebook, flipping back and forth, murmuring in German.

"You can't be serious." She crossed her arms and scowled. "Absolute nonsense."

Fischer chuckled.

"Open your mind. It's a grimoire. Like the *Grimorium Verum; The Book of Shadows;* or *The Lesser Key of Solomon.* Those are tomes of pure magic. What is contained *herein* is clearly an incomplete fusion of the occult and science. The foundation of their artistic identity and the emergent, tottering steps toward a coherent ritual. If their sequence of albums is an indicator, it might be known as *The Book of the Void.*"

He pushed the notebook to me with a solemn nod. We shared forbidden knowledge and thus were bonded.

At this point, the examination of the journal took on aspects of a sleepover when the children gather to spin campfire ghost stories, screw around with a Ouija board, and such. Frivolous, yet subtly tense. I unfolded my reading glasses and peered closely at fragmented excerpts, bits of arcane doggerel. These snatches of writing were sandwiched between vast spaces of indecipherable alchemical symbols and columns of musical notations. An undated passage written in the margins snagged my attention.

R made a lyre (chordophone) of antelope horns, catgut, and a greened pelvis bone. It can't get into a house where there's love and light. It has to wait outside in the dark, in the cold. We played the lyre and kept it at bay until dawn.

One summer, halcyon, I rode Godzilla over the meridian and you flew Rodan down from a black bell of dust, whoop-rattle-roll, everybody got irradiated, everybody died, everybody rose from the dead for the rematch. Today the man in the crow's robe gave you 25 to life. I took your wife home and fucked her. Vile powers judged. Undulant gods, Roko's Basilisk, music of the spheres, the infinite star-fucked gates flang wyde. Praise the parasite minds. Lern to dye so you might live proper. Descend into the galleries where night reigns eternal. Sing to the granite mirror and its echoes will carry down through the sunless mazes. Gaze into the Black Kaleidoscope…

I flinched at the sight of the Black Kaleidoscope. It

was a term used by a circle of aggressively devout UFO researchers I'd met on another case, and one I'd seen with increasing frequency. Birds of a feather pursued crackpot science together. The rub was, sometimes those crackpots, those true believers, weren't above getting their sacrificial daggers wet. Another detail of note—someone had scrawled a handful of regional maps highlighting Anvil Mountain and Harpy Peak. These landmarks were separated by thirty miles of rough terrain. The cartographer connected them with a double headed arrow. Harpy Peak was a mystery to me, but I knew precisely enough about Anvil Mountain to stay the hell clear. Wormy heart of cautionary legends predating the invasion of white colonists, it sat atop a system of unexplored caverns. I'd learned of its malevolent nature while locking horns with Zircon Corp who conducted secretive operations within its shadow. "Evil begets evil" has real-world applications.

Toward the end of the manuscript was an ink sketch techno-ouroboros, almost, but not quite, biting its tail. I'd seen iterations of the monster in the waking world and nightmares. Beneath the ouroboros in caps: PLANETARY LIGHTS-OUT SWITCH. HORSEHEADS, NY.

"The Barnhouses consulted on the supercollider," Fischer said when he noticed I'd lingered upon the image. "Funding fell through and the government didn't finish construction. Sandy, what was it again?"

THE WIND BEGAN TO HOWL

"The Jeffers Large Collider Project," I said. Far west of our current position; larger than life in my memory.

"You know of it, huh?"

"I investigated a suicide that occurred onsite shortly before the government pulled the plug." I'd earned powerful enemies during the course of my inquiries, chiefly Gerald Redlick, an industrial tycoon and founder of Redlick Group. Senator Redlick, now. "An army worked the collider. Hundreds and hundreds of specialists and consultants. Scientists, engineers, electricians. Thousands of laborers. What did a folk-rock duo have to offer? Morale? Entertainment?"

"Please, my prodigious friend," Fischer said. "Surely you've the imagination to understand the simple fact: artists provide a humanizing perspective to research projects, an element of creativity lacking in hidebound minds. The Barnhouses are experts in harmonics and acoustics. They are seekers."

I asked Krystal whether Harms arranged the supercollider gig for her friends. She pondered and said, possibly. Why did I ask? No reason, I said. Truth was, I'd begun to speculate on cabbages and kings and how an aging intelligence agent kept the rent paid on a New York apartment and professional goons on retainer. Serving as a ronin and headhunter for megacorporations such as Zircon and Redlick Group would do nicely. I mulled this while endeavoring to decipher the Barnhouse journal.

To the cynical, doggedly rational side of me, the journal entries resembled a tangle of sophomoric mumbo-jumbo produced by a pair of pothead college students. Any link to my previous misadventures was sheer happenstance. The caveman aspect that emerged after I bolted the doors at night was less dismissive. He didn't believe in coincidences. The weight of five years of creepy, unsettling experiences piled onto my shoulders like my own shadow transforming into an event horizon. I snatched my glass and gulped it down.

Gil returned to see why we'd gathered like cabalists around the table. He thumbed the bleary, faded pages. I was curious at what he might add to our speculation. This sort of hokum lay within the director's wheelhouse, given his mania for Clark Ashton Smith, psycho string charts, and slicing up screenplay drafts and gluing them together again with rubber cement.

"Fuckin' rad." He swilled from the neck of the Suntory bottle.

As the evening wound to its conclusion, I went onto the porch to clear my head in a rising north breeze. Texted Meg to let her know we'd survived the trip. Lionel seized the opportunity to extricate himself from the scene and join me. He lit another cigarette in a chain stretching back to a few bleak seconds after

THE WIND BEGAN TO HOWL

he'd awakened. Fischer and Gil had resumed a debate about the Catskill Devil. Krystal laughed, sufficiently drunk to cast off her resentment, and Billy Joel sang, all of it muffled by the log walls.

"*Is* there a Catskill Devil?" I asked after a while. By unspoken agreement, we weren't going to broach the weird stuff in the Barnhouse notebook, especially anything to with Anvil Mountain, black kaleidoscopes, or killer supercolliders.

"Beats me," Lionel said. "What I do know—somewhere there's an actor baking on a yacht in the Mediterranean, whining because he doesn't like a line in the latest script his agent sent by courier. And there's another guy who's lived in a ditch in an African or Middle Eastern nation for the past week and is down to his last three bullets."

"The rich actor will probably win an Oscar for portraying the resistance fighter. Speaking of Krystal…"

"What, no. She might murder Fischer in his sleep."

"She's kicking it to you."

Too dark to tell if he flushed.

"Lady already has more man action than she can handle."

"Oh, I think she's holding it down. Maybe you're the change-of-pace pitcher."

"I'm with Delia."

Again with his heiress flame, to my annoyance. Her daddy owned a controlling stake in Zircon Corp, one of the companies Urban mentioned. Not quite baddies, not quite goodies either. They considered me a bur under their collective saddle.

"You're not with Delia."

"Am so."

"Booty calls are not the basis of stable relationships," I said. "Delia's with that Motley Crüe-looking sonofabitch." The Motley-Crüe-looking sonofabitch played guitar for a world-famous rock band.

"They're not together-together."

"Did you miss the engagement ring? They're knocking boots in the Pyrenees. Doing the horizontal tango on Lake Tahoe. Double-back beasting at Shakespeare in the Park. Each other's plus one to Satanic orgies."

He crushed his cigarette butt under his heel.

"It's complicated."

"It's not complicated. You're a sap. Move along, little dogie."

His knuckles cracked.

We stood there not talking for a while, perilously close to exchanging blows. I waited for the pressure to ease. It did. He slapped my shoulder and stumbled inside.

Minerva snuffled, head tilted back. Whatever she whiffed displeased her.

"What if Harms isn't searching for the Barnhouses?" I asked her, the glittering stars. "Suppose he already has them?" And if that were the case, I'd tipped my hand when I left a message for him the other day.

THE WIND BEGAN TO HOWL

She crouched upon my feet, growling. In a previous life, she'd been my wolf.

The middle of the night flowed from its bottomless well. I left my bunk to eat more pills and let Minerva run. A cool, powerful wind descended upon the valley, thrashing the hell out of the pines and the sheds. Twigs and needles pinged off the shutters. Green odors of the deep forest eddied forth—rotten wood, moss, and loam, and fruiting carcasses. The litany of moans and grinding branches was expected, but as I stood, listening to the wind and shining my flashlight around, trying to spotlight Minerva, metallic chiming resounded somewhere in the south forty. Aboverose the throaty cry of an animal I didn't recognize, brought across the gulf to me by shivery gusts. An aggrieved sobbing uttered miles off down a gulch, or a mere fifty paces through the primeval dark. Minerva came flying like a bat out of hell and I followed her, spear in one hand, torch guttering in the other, back into our cave. I rested awhile near the wan glow of the hearth, senses attuned to what thrummed beneath the howling storm. All the genetically transmitted superstition of the world concentrated itself within my fast-beating heart. Thought perhaps I was privileged, or damned, to apprehend the Manitou's cry woven into the tumult. Those chimes rose and fell, dinging and lost. Minerva stirred, head cocked as if a dangerous presence passed too near our shelter. A slouching shadow of doom that has stalked man and dog since we first huddled together in the fire's glow. The sun rose, red and sullen. Black specks of angels or devils wheeled in its shimmering lens.

CHAPTER TWELVE
(Descent Upon Harpy's Glen)

Breakfast was a muted affair. Everybody except Fischer contended with a crippling hangover. Eggs, toast, coffee, and lots of tomato juice. My plans to sally forth early were derailed; we didn't escape the gravity well of the cabin and our communal misery until noon.

It was agreed to divide the search. Lionel and Krystal joined me and Minerva for a trip to Harpy's Glen. Fischer and Urban reconnoitered nearby Helmwood. Gil chose his poison and accompanied them. I prayed to the gods my traveling companions wouldn't become immediately embroiled in a discussion concerning sex magic, gnostic traditions, and alien abductions.

It went another, only marginally less predictable direction.

Krystal said, "I'm a pushover for classic movie posters of ugly movie stars. Bogart. Ernest Borgnine.

Toshiro Mifune." She'd been maniacally cheerful all morning. Fischer had afforded her a wide berth.

Lionel scoffed.

"The hell you say. Mifune was a handsome sonofagun."

"Unshaven Henry Fonda in *Once Upon a Time in the West?*"

"Madness, lady. Fonda was a gorgeous, gorgeous man."

"James Coburn. Woody Strode. Charles Bronson."

"*Those* were some squinty-eyed, sweaty hombres," he said.

"Sexy in their own special way."

"Eli Wallach?"

"Take me now, baby!" Krystal fanned herself.

I'd chosen Harpy's Glen based upon the fact Krystal and the Barnhouses had knocked around its precincts in times gone by. I'd encouraged the other members of the "fellowship" to head elsewhere simply to keep them occupied. The brothers had played numerous gigs in the region, including the Harpy Tavern. I couldn't imagine their funky stylings soothed savage breasts in these parts. Neither were my hopes high that we'd acquire a solid lead. Mainly because in these types of investigations, reliable information was a rare commodity and a product of legwork, drudgery, and time. Nonetheless, there was always a chance someone remembered them or knew of the studio. With a moniker like Wails and Moans, I hoped a local might be able to at least point in the general direction.

THE WIND BEGAN TO HOWL

The town of seven hundred occupied a wooded valley several miles west of Harpy Peak. So sleepy as to be comatose, although built to revive during ski season. On Main Street I catalogued a church, post office, hair salon, diner, general store, antique shop, winter gear outlet, and hardware store. Some frontage space had FOR RENT signs in the windows. The Nest Tavern waited one street over; closed until 2 P.M. I decided it wouldn't be worth traipsing into until sundown brought forth a crowd of thirsty woods folk. A bit farther down the side street was the Glen Inn, a charming three-story peak-roof building that served as overflow for the Harpy Peak Resort. I began canvassing at one end of the main drag; Lionel and Krystal handled the opposite side.

I leashed Minerva to a bike rack and strolled into the salon. The resident stylist wasn't enthused by my appearance—and me decked out in a suit jacket, slacks, and spit-shined leather lace-up boots. She saw nothing, knew nothing. Same deal with the denizens of the antique shop and hardware store. I'd conceded defeat in eliciting a response from the clerk when an older, silvery-haired man who doubtless voted Republican banged through the door of a storage room. I gathered he'd eavesdropped on my conversation with his subordinate. He said, skedaddle, it ain't ski season, boy! And supplemented this order with an or else, indicating the PREMISES INSURED BY SMITH & WESSON sign prominently displayed at the entrance. A broad-shouldered patron in logging duds stepped around the corner to back the owner's play with a mean mug dialed to ten. I skedaddled.

Undaunted, I barged into the diner. The lone waitress rebuffed me sweetly and brought a cup of pretty decent coffee, which I drank while observing my dog through the window. Trained and drilled with the efficiency of a special forces soldier, Minerva didn't require restraints, but people fear unleashed dogs. There were three patrons in the diner—a guy at the counter arguing football history with the fry cook on the other side of the service window; and two men eating lunch at the same table, each walled off behind a newspaper. A photograph of Harpy Peak, circa 1976, hung over a door to the restrooms. I asked the waitress if business picked up and she said, yeah, December. My phone buzzed and it was Meg on the line, which alarmed me for a second, imagining the worst as we tended to confine our communication to evenings, but she was calling to check that I hadn't died of a concussion and whether her Caravan was in one piece. I said camp scared me and creepy events were afoot, could I come home early? Meg promised Minerva would protect me, she had to go—her boss would be along any second. We hung up and I stared at the screen, thinking, hilarious quip, since she was her own boss at the new library post. Suddenly hungry, I ordered a cheeseburger. The waitress asked how I wanted it and I said, same color as my face. The lady nodded solemnly and scribbled on a ticket.

I'd put away the better half of lunch when Lionel

THE WIND BEGAN TO HOWL

and Krystal clinked the bell over the door. Her cheeks were rosy. He was still hungover.

"Nobody but nobody has jack or shit to say," he said. She cleared her throat. He sighed. "Well, a couple of them talked to her. Or babbled in tongues while they ogled."

"Got to know how to ask." She rebuttoned the second button on her low-cut blouse. She nabbed a fry off my plate. "Oooh, greasy spoon fries! Mind if I…?"

I wrapped the last of the fries in a napkin and saved them for Minerva, the Fry Eating Champion.

"What's the verdict? Any luck? I've only scared the fish."

Krystal said, "The name Barnhouse draws a blank in neighborhood businesses."

"A dearth of art lovers?"

"Local elders prefer jug bands and the youngsters aren't hip to brown noise by way of Jethro Tull. What are ya gonna do?"

"None of them heard of Wails and Moans?"

"Alas, no," she said.

"They wished they had." He inclined his head toward her and sketched an hourglass mid-air. "It's on one a them thar hills, for sure! We've canvassed Main Street and the tavern isn't open yet." No mistaking his expression; my comrade had set his heart on a midafternoon bender. He regarded his palm as if reading a letter. "Dearest, Martha, as autumn, then killing winter draw near, I fear our prospects are increasingly hopeless."

"Hold on, amigo. Those fabled doors will soon swing wide. Perhaps we should visit yon inn. The rosy-cheeked innkeeper may have heard rumors of rumors." I paid with a card and tucked a generous gratuity under my waterglass. I walked outside, marveling at how the buildings and the street appeared to simply end where the surrounding greenery began. Minerva wagged her entire body as I approached; she could smell a fry from another county.

Next stop, the Glen Inn. Had to be a new building, but I tipped my hat to the architect and the construction company who put it together in the style of a faux colonial mansion, complete with a patina of Nathaniel Hawthorne authenticity.

"Gables!" Krystal clapped and dug into Lionel with her elbow.

"When you're right, you're right," he said. "Who doesn't love gables?"

I hitched Minerva and walked inside. The entry parlor smelled piney. It featured a gas hearth, fancy couches, overstuffed chairs, and more pictures of Harpy Peak in the raw, and a sequence of skiers assaying the slopes. Sweet lighting—whoever managed the hotel fully understood the art of floor and accent lamps. The walnut reception counter was buffed to a high gloss.

The desk clerk eyed me. Took swift inventory, and smiled. Youngish, trim in his suit and Lennon glasses. His tag said James.

THE WIND BEGAN TO HOWL

"Hi, welcome to the Glen Inn."

Normally, I don't lead with my business card as it can put functionaries off their feed. Hotel clerks are built different. Daytime staff loathe their superiors and nighttime staff seldom have a solitary fuck to give. I hoped this person would at least occupy the middle ground. Maybe I flexed as I leaned on the counter and asked if he'd heard of the Barnhouses or Wails and Moans.

Once he realized I wasn't a potential patron or a cop, aloof professionalism went right out the window.

"Huh, a real live private detective. Would've guessed boxer."

"Punching bag, maybe. What have you got for me, Jimmy?"

"Already to pet names, are we? Well, tall, dark, and tenderized, I'm newly transplanted from Coxsackie. 'Whispers and Moans' was a Crowded House single before I was born, and the only Barnhouse I'm familiar with is an eccentric scientist on the run in a Vonnegut short story."

"*Wails* and Moans. We'll let it slide. Life imitates art. Everybody is looking for my Barnhouses too. Best if I find them first."

"Black hats on their trail?"

I pointed to the nastier of my two shiners.

"The black hats did this to my beautiful face."

He nodded toward Lionel.

"Same baddies smack him around?"

"No, he ran into a door."

"Uh-huh. Unfortunately, I can't help. Are you in town for the evening?"

"Easy, tiger. We have a cabin."

I peeled a twenty off my roll and pressed it into his palm. Urged him to call me if he remembered anything useful.

"You're welcome to rest in our lobby," James said. "I'll bring a coffee service. Hand-ground Columbian blend."

"Your offer is gratefully accepted." My back was killing me.

We adjourned to a window table. A fine view of the trees. All of them. Presently James brought a carafe of coffee and a tray of sugar cookies, doubtless imported from some bakery in Kingston or Oneonta.

Lionel removed his shooting glasses. He bit into a cookie. He sipped his coffee.

"Okay cookie," he said drolly. "Damned good coffee."

Krystal laughed. She asked James if there were any sights we should visit as he passed around full-color brochures.

"Lake Terron, fifteen minutes west. Otherwise known as Lake Terror."

"Why Lake Terror?"

"Because kids are grandiose? Onward to Owl Falls. Lovely picnic spot if you can handle a three-mile hike. Harpy Peak Museum. Head for the resort;

THE WIND BEGAN TO HOWL

it's on the road. Nothing exciting. A glorified tourist shop. Allegedly there are bunkers sunk into some of the hills—eccentric rich folks were into bomb shelter culture in the '50s and '60s."

"True!" Krystal said. "The Catskills and Adirondacks would be ideal biomes to survive a nuclear holocaust."

"Sparkling clear irradiated mountain streams," Gil said.

"And Killjack Mine," James continued placidly. "Open from 11 A.M. until 5 P.M., Monday through Friday. Memorabilia, refreshments, and three guided tours daily. Lots of mines and caves in these parts. Prospect Mine, Killjack Caverns, Green Reaper Caves. Killjack Mine is the only safe one." The clerk paused. "If you're lucky, you'll get the Singing Guide. She yodels in the mine tunnels, tells ghost stories, recites Appalachian poetry. I did the tour with her. Very cool."

"You made it back alive," I said. "There's an endorsement."

"Why I qualified the coolness."

We killed an hour-and-a-half, enjoying coffee and cookies while avoiding the topic of the errant rockers. Gil sent a message reporting a lack of success in Helmwood. He and his party planned to have dinner, make the rounds of the restaurant and tavern, then meet us at the cabin for a nightcap.

Lionel consulted his watch.

"Beer-thirty."

Out the window, curbside shadows stretched, cruel and skeletal. No longer sneaking, but coming in a jumbled rush.

Minerva barked. She only barked when guarding the house or a vehicle, or if she'd spotted a threat. Her bear and coyote bark. Her bad person bark. This was new. Almost an aggrieved screech. I was through the hotel door and into the street without clear recollection of leaving the table. Lionel left me in the dust.

CHAPTER THIRTEEN
(The Seven-League Step)

A hillbilly loomed on the sidewalk; troll-like in a mangy gray coat, wool pants, and unlaced combat boots. His crooked ballcap (flecked with blood, if I wasn't mistaken) and a snaggly salt-and-pepper beard lent him a saturnine eminence, as if a figure of folklore had burst from the forest depths to bestow rough-spun wisdom or exact bloody retribution. He was Goya's Saturn glaring down upon my hound leashed to a newspaper box. Minerva snapped and cowered; terrified, yet unwilling to permit him to enter the hotel. My faithful girl.

Lionel assessed the situation in a heartbeat. He'd square up against anyone without blinking. He sighed and snicked open a pocket knife against his pant leg. He walked toward the hillbilly.

"A fact you may find pertinent," he said to the man. "Everybody's the same height lying down."

"Wait, wait," Krystal said in a higher pitch than

usual. Her dazed expression was of someone slowly rousing while a dream kept looping in the background. "Roger!" Her emotion wasn't as joyful as one might've expected.

She was right—here stood Roger Barnhouse in the flesh, and more so. Gaunter and seedier than the photos. An imposing composite of images.

He said to her, "Hi, darling." And to me, "It's okay. Tell your dog it's okay." And to Lionel, "Blondie, it's okay." His teeth were mismatched and stained yellow. A mouth to swallow infants whole or stones in swaddling linens, or a brave, hapless dog. The man leaned way over and held his grimy hand before Minerva's snout and she didn't bite him.

Lionel straightened. He disappeared the knife into his pocket.

Krystal ran toward her boyfriend, froze as if reconsidering, then went to him and threw her arms around his neck.

"What in the hell are you doing here? You're not supposed—" She pushed herself away. "Bastard! Where's Ken?" No kiss, only recriminations.

"Sends his love. I'm thirsty. You folks thirsty?"

Stars drilled through the suddenly black sky. Neon fizzed: THE NEST. I stumbled, the way you do when the end of the escalator comes as a surprise.

"Bring her in," Roger said as I cast about for somewhere to hitch Minerva. "The bartender won't give you any static." His gangly arm wrapped around

Krystal's waist. Her expression was happy; glazed smile, entranced.

Dim inside—lofty roof, creaky little tables, yet more black and white photos of forbidding peaks and mustachioed loggers. Jukebox, pool table, shuffleboard. Quiet, but locals were drifting in. Plaid, denim, leather. The bartender filled two pitchers of draft suds and another of tap water. He turned a blind eye to the formidable dog in his establishment, but a salt of the earth galoot at the pool table didn't exercise discretion.

Pool Jockey eyeballed Minerva. He shook his head.

"Whoa. Read the sign. No. Fucking. Dogs."

I poured water into a glass for Minerva.

"Strike two."

"Strike two?"

"Your face is strike one."

Roger's turn to play Kissinger.

He said, "Rest your lips, friend. These gentlemen will slit your throat soon as look at you."

Pool Jockey squinted.

"Oh, hell, Rog. Didn't see you standing there. Yeah, no problem." He promptly resumed minding his own business.

Lionel placed quarters on the edge of the pool table and smiled at Pool Jockey with the intensity of a gunfighter challenging his rival to a high noon throw down.

"He didn't see you standing there?" I said. "All seven feet of you."

Roger smiled a sadly menacing smile.

"I cloud the minds of men when it suits me. And women," he said under his breath as Krystal sat next to him. "You've come to propose a bargain."

"To enforce a bargain. Your pal, Gil Finlay is in a bind. He—well, his lawyers—need you and your brother to sign a contract. Boilerplate, but it has to be done. I'm the process server."

"We told Gil he could borrow the song. Nobody can sue him for infringement except for me or Ken. He's in the clear."

"The lawyers disagree."

"Those scoundrels and scoundrels like them have dogged our trail since forever. Lawyer is another word for adversary. Adversary is long for Satan. Boilerplate is seldom boilerplate. I'll decline."

"I must insist."

"Boys, can't we have a nice peaceful drink?" Krystal said.

The musician fished rolling papers and tobacco from his coat.

"Alas, Messrs. Clupach, Ransom, and Friend are a day late and a dollar short." He rolled a cigarette.

"You're a writer." I instinctively sought a different angle. "Novelist, troubadour, magician."

His features knurled and shifted like a thunderhead.

"I have written."

NO SMOKING signs in prominent locations; he lit his cigarette with a match, and puffed. Smoke rolled

THE WIND BEGAN TO HOWL

at me, prickling with forks of lightning. Washed over and through me and I got a whiff of burning pine, scorched hide, blood, and bone.

"Druid fire courses in my veins and now it does in yours too," he said. "Once this gets in your lungs, stitching thought together is hard, locomotion is impossible. You'll have to shadow walk, fly the astral realms on a silver cord into the sunless depths. The silver cord is the twine that courageous, demented Theseus carried into the Minotaur's labyrinth. A man will do anything to get fucked, won't he? Well, so will a bull."

Krystal coughed demurely.

Roger said to her, "Honey, be an angel and go hustle blondie while I chat with Lurch here?" He watched her sashay toward Lionel as if he'd wound her spring and set her loose. He filled our mugs and had a swallow. "She's a spy in the house of love, yet an innocent. Her perfidy is akin to yours. Bumbling, artless as a child. I'd prefer to maintain the illusion of decency, of familial tenderness. Understand? The necessity of shielding loved ones from our true nature?"

I understood. Oh, how I understood.

He said, "You've tangled with my kind."

"What kind are you, Barnhouse?"

Meanwhile, Lionel prepared to break. He scowled.

"Why does this felt smell like piss?"

"Take a guess!" Krystal perched upon a stool, beer bottle in hand.

Roger's thick glasses glimmered with trapped suns.

"Amidst the penny-ante betrayals, blackmail, and redneck skullduggery, you've glimpsed true evil. The corporate spy turned serial killer you put in the ground? He jumpstarted his career of evil testing weapons for the DoD. The freaks in Horseheads and their cult leader? Zircon Corp and Senator Redlick? Haven't you gotten an inkling that you're involved, enmeshed, in a larger pattern? There are no coincidences."

"You've been reading my mail," I said with false calm. No logical way for him to be privy to these details, a couple of which might land me in hot water were the authorities to become wise.

"Genius loci, friend. I'm the spirit of the place now, more or less. You and I are members of an exclusive club. Material existence resides inside the nucleus of a cell, ad infinitum. Which is why Tom Bombadil reigns supreme in *The Lord of the Rings.* The thunder of the heavens. The woodsmoke in the dale. The crackling of a volcano. His song is doom to the living dead. He's elite. I'm almost elite. You might get there."

Lionel said from a thousand miles away, "Hey, I was just talking about—"

"Yeah, buddy," the musician said. "Isaiah Coleridge." He cleared his throat and pronounced my name with a ritualistic flourish. Priests and wizards supposedly name devils summoned to a magic circle. It gives them power over their subject. "Mind if I bend your ear? Turn on your phone, record this for posterity."

"Oh, was that preamble?" But I set my phone on the table. Heavy as a rock.

Whatever laced the smoke worked fast. The lamps and jukebox lights softened and dulled, softened, and sputtered, softened and softened. I gripped the arms of my chair to avoid sliding into outer space. The iron band of an invisible circle tightened around my shoulders and thighs. Fleeting bits of my consciousness observed this could be the effects of a sedative combined with hypnotic suggestion. I'd been drugged, poisoned, and mind-fucked before and recognized the symptoms. The most insidious aspect? I couldn't muster fear, not even an iota of righteous indignation.

The pool table floated overhead; an island of gauzy light. Roger and I, Minerva underfoot, were suspended in an oubliette. Everything and everyone else vanished into the haze. Linda Ronstadt's voice sang far across the sea. Sirens of the deep were her chorus.

He said, "Ken and I were raised in the boondocks. Owned a whole library of regular books, and almanacs, an encyclopedia set, medical and veterinarian texts, and those thick sonsofbitches about engineering and history. Saved my life. Saved Ken's life. The old man took us hunting and his real love—caving. No musician, he possessed a knack for whistling. Whistled whole complicated songs; if he heard it on the radio or TV, he could whistle it like a pro. Down in the caves, we'd gather, utterly blind, and listen to him whistle, listen to the tunnels and chimneys carry his melodies, warped and changing as they drifted, then silence. He's the one who taught us there's potency in harmonics, in phrases and intonations. Rituals.

"My eighteenth birthday, I enlisted with the Army and my father, on his last legs from cirrhosis, bid me good riddance the way *his* father signed a paper and shipped him off to Vietnam. Burned four years of my life. Yeah, I saw action. Shot three Hadjis in an ambush. Blew another enemy soldier up with an improvised boobytrap. Followed a trail of blood and pieces of meat. The trail ended in scrub where a breeze shivered the stalks, riffing in a black wave toward the setting sun and infinity. A voice spoke to me from the scrub and the rocks bordering the scrub. The voice of my father, but kindly. I resisted the urge to answer. Heard versions of that voice again. The voice of Mom, dead of an embolism or a broken heart, the voice of a comrade who'd gotten fragged. The dead whispered. Sometimes on the cusp of sleep, or while bent to change a tire, or deal a hand of Five Card Stud, or when I stroked toward conclusion as a lover moaned, her features soft and changeable as warm clay.

Walk on out here. I miss you, son.

"Ken also suffered demons. Went harder for him, the delicate one. Where does a man put such weird experiences? What does a man do with restless ghosts?

You chase them in circles and go madder by the day, or you corral them in a mental lockbox and toss the key. The Army didn't fill the hole at the center of our beings. Excavated it deeper. Ken and I fell back into the childhood pit after our service. Parents dead. Meaningful connections severed. We wandered, aimless as ronin. Fucking. Fighting. Would've gone on until something terrible happened. Something terrible *did* happen. We failed to realize its scope.

"Cordell Harms came to our rescue. Cordell was tender to me and Ken in a way our own father couldn't be. Encouraged the formation of the Barnhouse writing duo, the musicians. Said he'd analyzed transcripts, psych profiles, and dossiers; he'd attended our high school talent shows and read my essay on Coltrane's *Circle of Tones*. He watched over us, a devilish guardian angel, waiting for the right moment to swoop in. We had to ripen, to season. To suffer and to visit suffering upon our enemies. The law of Shakespeare prevails. Turns out, he was the enemy waiting for us at home. The minotaur at the end of the labyrinth." He reached over and powered off my phone.

"Roger…why…your…life…story?" An eon elapsed between the first and last syllable.

He inhaled and the cherry of his cigarette flared. Flakes of ash turned in zero-g; the dying sparks of a vast forest fire sucked into a vacuum.

"My greatest mistake, and Ken's, was to trust Cordell Harms. Our doom was to sever the bonds of servitude, to shed the manacles he'd tightened and tightened. Why the story? To set the table. It's your story too, Isaiah. *You* came after us. *You* opened the door. So let us walk across the threshold. Fuck Cordell. Fuck Gil and sweet Krystal. Fuck those damned lawyers who'd make us galley slaves rowing to hell."

The lamp hissed and snarled at a frequency so low it bubbled in my blood. It was a receding star. Hercules, Alpha Centauri, Nemesis. My heart slowed, slowed, thickened with frozen motor oil. Terror winged toward me across the vast, dead void, but dinosaurs would live and die again before it swept over me in an obliterating wave.

I tried to speak further, to demand an explanation, to ask why he was talking like a fortune cookie. Instead, I emitted the hiss of cosmic background radiation. The circuits between my brain and my mouth were offline.

Roger grinned. Tar overflowed and oozed into his beard. It wasn't Green Apple chaw or Copenhagen. He gagged and a clod of wet soil plopped onto the table.

"You're close to El Dorado, Shangri-La. Wails and Moans. Come loaded for bear. I repeat: put on your armor, strap on your sword. Gird them loins. It'll be root hog or die. Not going to give you the address. I've seen the likely possible outcomes. Nothing changes for me or Ken. You and your merry band have a little more riding on the consequences of choice. Go tonight, in the dark, you'll die for certain. Get some sleep, be a detective tomorrow, and the light of revelation will surely dawn."

He rose and hunched to avoid smashing his skull into the ceiling.

"Ever notice how it isn't your fate to save anyone? You're no rescuer, no savior. You're the custodian of the gods. Sometimes you let blood; sometimes you come along with a mop. Hurry. You don't have time to change the black sails."

The balladeer, the trickster, the agent of night, strode toward and through the wall into a starfield. His image glitched, became an upside down negative, and dissolved. The lights came up. Rowdy laughter and chatter of a drunken crowd boomed the way commercials crash in after the credits of a muted TV program. Minerva pressed her muzzle into my shin, quaking.

CHAPTER FOURTEEN
(Snip the Silver Cord)

The invisible shackles released and I was on my feet, careening among startled patrons. The wall was solid. I veered and shouldered aside the door. Crisp, cool air. Shop fronts were empty as glass eyes. Leaf-scent and bark replaced booze and tobacco fumes. Dark sky streaked red where it rolled into infinity. I recovered, paid the tab, and gathered my associates for the drive home. Lionel and Krystal were sufficiently in their cups that I pulled my act together and took the wheel. Night on those strange roads caused the trip to drag. Silence dragged too, until Krystal burst into tears. Delayed reaction to stress.

"There's a black hole where he stood." She tapped her forehead. "I see you and the table. I see his smoke. He's a black hole. Nothing there in my mind." More heartbroken sobs. "You let him leave." Her face was luminous in the mirror, seeming to float in the dimness of the interior, shining with hatred. "You let him? Why?"

Lionel didn't make any effort to comfort her. He lit a cigarette. Rolled the window down and exhaled. I figured he was keeping tabs on the headlights behind our vehicle. A local drunk toddling home, or an enemy tracking us to the cabin. Time would tell. I turned onto the dirt road and the trailing rig zoomed past. Minerva curled tight on the front passenger seat, whimpering. It occurred to me that she might've ingested a secondhand dose of the stuff Roger was puffing. I clucked at her and she raised her head, alert.

Somebody had a lantern blazing on the porch to guide us in. Smoking and playing poker, Gil, Fischer, and Urban greeted our arrival with huzzahs. Krystal flopped down beside them and Fischer dealt her in to a hand of Five Card Draw.

Lionel and I held a private confab on the porch. He listened and smoked. I massaged my temples, analyzing my conversation with Roger Barnhouse as dryly and rationally as possible.

"Barnhouse walked through a wall," was my summary.

"Dude walked out the front door."

I considered and discarded several retorts.

"Okay, fine. Barnhouse must've slipped a mickey in the beer, loaded his tobacco with weapons-grade hallucinogens. I was dosed."

"You didn't get him to sign the papers."

"Needless to say, no."

THE WIND BEGAN TO HOWL

"Any line on where his brother is, or where they're shacked up?"

"The conversation didn't lead that direction."

Another gusty exhalation.

"He wasn't *talking*."

I played the recording on my phone. Bar chatter and the jukebox blasting didn't help the sound quality. Thirty seconds in, I stopped.

"He's chanting. And it's…"

"Fucking backwards."

"Backwards. Creepy as the results may be, we'll save the conclusion of witchcraft. Electronic devices are vulnerable to manipulation."

"He touched your phone."

"Exactly. Magnetism or similar effect."

"Everyone claims the Barnhouses are masters of closeup magic," Lionel said. "Sleight of hand. He zaps your phone with a magnet, or messes with its functions, reprograms it. I dunno."

"Answering that question leads to the next—what's his motive?" Neither of us could solve the riddle. Already, details were blurring at the edges. Barnhouse's face distorted in my memory, melting wax.

Finally, Lionel said, "How now? Pack our shit and vamoose? I'm partial to vamoosing. Missing my own squalid pad, y'know?"

"We're paid up through Sunday. Do what we do until then."

"Dig?"

"Dig."

"Isaiah, what's the point? If we find him and his bro again, so what? Gonna screw a revolver barrel in his ear and force him to sign?" He studied me. "Goddamn it. You're in Lee Van Cleef mode. You always see the job through."

He was on the money. To hell with the day rate and the bonus. Daredevils leap from planes for the rush. Adventurous souls die on mountains because the mountains are there. I'm uncompromising in my own unique way—somebody fucks around with me, they're bound to find out.

I called Meg and chatted with her and Devlin who greeted me with a gurgling cry. Meg said the boy had rampaged around the house since sunup practicing Wilhelm screams at varying decibels. School would resume next week and that nagged at my conscience; I needed to get myself home and pitch in. She detected tension in my voice and asked if I was okay. Better than, I assured her. Spent a while on the porch looking at the stars. Looking for unknown headlights on the secluded lane, or among the trees. I dwelled on Roger Barnhouse's febrile countenance, the dirt crumbling from his lips.

Gil and the others were dumbfounded when I explained meeting Roger Barnhouse at the tavern. I omitted the details. They asked a bunch of questions I couldn't answer, except to say we'd head home on Sunday. The drinking resumed. Ghost stories, tall tales. I listened to Urban and Gil hold court. Krystal withdrew to the side, wan and shaken.

Lying in the bunk, shadows smothered me. Each replay of the surreal conversation with Roger Barnhouse warped farther from baseline reality. Him singing, not speaking. Screaming, not singing. Rivulets of mud poured over his face; a corroded stalactite pierced the top of his skull.

Too much. Sweat-soaked, I frantically shed the devil-sent homunculus crouched upon my chest and went into the main room. Clicked on a solitary lamp and poured whiskey so fast it sloshed over the rim of the glass. Gulped three of those and beheld my hideous expression smeared in the window pane. May as well have been a midnight ghoul leering around the corner of a tombstone.

Friday and Saturday were divided between canvassing Wilder and Smith Town. We enjoyed the rustic glories on offer—decent food, beautiful geography, quaint and colorful folk—but learned nothing to aid our cause. Supplies were running low. I gave a short speech: we'd head toward more civilized climes the following day; thanks for the companionship, this was, sadly, a typical chapter in the annals of a detective. Blind alleys and a bar bill. After the company retired, I hunkered by the fire,

Minerva curled at my feet, and pored over *The Book of the Void*. An empty gesture, akin to picking at wounds. The Barnhouse case hurt, thus I embraced it with a masochistic fervor. If you can't fix a problem, you *can* seek catharsis by making the whole damned thing worse and worse. Flip the checker board, kick the sandcastle, et cetera.

Gil rustled a final hurrah banquet. We ate and made merry, as such merriment was to be had, and killed the remnants of booze. The prevailing mood waxed somber—a summer vacation ending on a downer note, nobody certain they shared the affections of fellow travelers.

Fischer guzzled quantities of beer and wine to put Lionel to shame. He'd obviously built his courage toward a confrontation the entire evening.

"Coleridge, Sandy inquired about you—"

"Hush!" Urban shuddered from drowsy repose, placed a finger against his lips, and hissed fiercely.

He caressed her hand and grinned at me, well and truly drunk at last. The cast-iron constitution of his had its limit.

"Her Agency friends are convinced you were a miscreant in the past."

Who knows what he expected? I wasn't easily baited in regard to my misspent youth.

"I'm a leopard. See my same spots."

"Hey, there's a Parcheesi board on the shelf," Gil said in an effort to broker peace. He didn't comprehend the extent of my wicked ways, but he knew Curtis and the kind of guys Curtis attracted into his orbit. No poker of bears, my pal Gil.

"Maybe you're a sociopath," Fischer said.

"Maybe it's Maybelline." Whenever someone is rude to me on the street, shoots me the bird in traffic, gives me lip or the hairy eyeball, I smile and take a sip of their soul. I smiled at him. "Too self-aware for a sociopath. Might have to accept the fact I'm a little bit evil."

"Aren't we all?" Urban said. "Ignore Stan. He considers himself an auteur, above compromise. Such is his privilege, to pass judgment in comfort and ease."

"Hey," Stan said, wounded.

I didn't care. Best that she'd backed him down before I hurt more than his feelings.

Soured, the group turned in early. I maintained my customary post-lights-out vigil, poring over the Barnhouse Codex. My name for the brothers' collaborative scribbles. Encountered this passage:

Dad shaved the warden's face clean off with a notched doublebit axe. His white bone death masque stared in grinning shock until red burst from its sockets. Daddy next whacked the trooper in a big overhead stroke like he was splitting a stump. Left the axe stuck in his skull. The pair had come onto the homestead together, so Dad buried them together. Dropped their Stratton hats into the hole, and their radios and guns, and then the dirt. Thirteen was too young to pull a trigger, but he allowed as I could handle a shovel. Fact was, I did most of the digging in the hard earth. When we returned to the house, it was almost daylight. Mama sat us at the table. Flapjacks and coffee. First time they gave me coffee.... If anybody ever came around hunting for the warden and the trooper, I didn't hear about it. This was autumn of Nineteen-Hundred and Seventy-Nine. Six months later, Dad upped stakes and moved the clan east.

Chilled me to the core. The highlights reminded me of my own blackhearted father, author of many similar dark deeds I am certain.

I listened to the audio of my conversation with Roger. Snatches of it, at least. It proved nigh fruitless attempting to cobble sense from a muddy phone recording of a guttural voice. As Gil had said, myth claimed rock and roll albums hid Satanic messages. I lived through that era. Rock songs weren't alone when it came to allegedly spreading hidden messages. I'd watched my share of paranormal TV wherein "researchers" claimed spirits communicated via reversed speech. This felt similar. An idea occurred to me—rather than recreate entire sentences, I tuned in to individual words and short phrases. Within a minute or two, I struck gold. *Cat Party.* Thinking back to the cat party in Rosendale, my impulse was to chuckle. Under different circumstances, sure. After more close listening, *Harley* coalesced. The name of one of the cats.

Skimming, I marked a dozen utterances of Harley. I cross-referenced the journal—two instances of Harley, both written backwards. Sobered me completely. There are no coincidences. Say it ad nauseam and it won't be any less true.

I rang the Glen Inn and the person who answered said James was off duty. They must've passed along the message, because James called back shortly. I asked if he'd heard of Harley, either a person or a place. No, he'd ask the staff, check back tomorrow.

The half-skull moon shined upon me as I tossed and turned on the couch. Bit by bit, its grin was damped. Roger Barnhouse's disembodied head replaced the moon and rolled across my dreamscapes, muttering a dirge. Whatever words accompanied the melody issued as a Gregorian chant. In reverse, naturally.

CHAPTER FIFTEEN
(Wails & Moans)

James texted bright and early with news about the location of the lost studio. This presented me with a decision—keep the information to myself or share with the group. For logistical reasons, I opted not to share. We ate breakfast, after which, Gil, Fischer, and Urban piled into their rig and lit out for Providence. Once they'd gone, I leveled with Krystal. One way or another, she deserved to be here with us at this moment of possible revelation.

Clouds obscured the peaks and veiled the road. Made for a slow drive down into the valley. I filled our tank in Harpy's Glen. James waved as he exited the station. He was dressed in a jean jacket and shades, cheap cup of coffee in hand.

"Hit me, dude," I said.

He said, "I've got swing shift, but I woke my sorry ass and went in special on your behalf. I'm pals with a maintenance man at the hotel. Old timer. Asked him about your studio, Whispers—Wails and Moans. He thought it sounded familiar. Place in the woods known as Harley House. Completely ruined after a winter storm and a fire two, three years ago, my colleague says. Has a bad reputation. Haunted, or a hobo den, I dunno. Folks tend to incorporate these landmarks into local mythology, then ignore them, by and large. The region has a history of city slickers gobbling swaths of land to build private getaways, museums, hunting lodges, you name it. There's an abandoned theme park..."

As the clerk spoke, a chill stole along my spine. In one stroke, he'd zeroed in on the Barnhouses' likely hidey hole. Detecting is either tedious or lethally simple. "Simple" solutions didn't exist in a practical sense. I'd been around the block; when everything falls into place of its own accord, the other shoe is bound to drop. On your head, and the shoe is an anvil.

I immediately studied the area map on my phone. Scattered neighborhoods, named creeks and copses, and a branch of the defunct Killjack Mine. Sure as taxes, an unidentified building sat atop a ridgeline roughly three-quarters of a mile due south of Harpy's Glen if one trekked directly over hill and dale. Or, the much longer route: indications were of a road or trail entering from the opposite side of a ridgeline. Nine-mile drive to reach the access point and no guarantee the unnamed road was navigable. A beeline it was, then.

THE WIND BEGAN TO HOWL

James gave me a meaningful eyebrow waggle.

"I do good?"

"Yeah, kid. You may have cracked the case." I passed him some folding green and he winked and departed. I said, "Anybody care to join me for an excursion?"

I parked two blocks over at the edge of town. Roger Barnhouse had said a few choice things; choicest being his admonition to come armed. Lionel donned a relatively compact Kevlar vest and grabbed the Mossberg. I shrugged into the heavy ballistic jacket. Ceramic plates made it decent as a bullet-stopper and a better-than-average defense against edged weapons.

Krystal frowned as we strapped into our armor. She became downright unhappy watching Lionel load the shotgun.

"I don't understand," she said. "Why the hunting gear?"

"Best to err on the side of overcaution," I said.

Lionel tried a reassuring smile.

"Go loaded for bear, you won't run into any bear. It's the opposite of Murphy's Law."

We located a well-trod footpath curving downslope into the woods in the general direction of the alleged Harley House. Birds yelled in dismay. After a few moments I realized they weren't screeching at our intrusion. Barometric pressure built in my skull. A shadow zipped past my peripheral vision. Lionel shifted the barrel of the shotgun. Minerva's ears pricked. Krystal gazed into her phone like it was a palantír. No apparent awareness by the others.

The trail rounded a bend and sloped downward to a dilapidated covered bridge. Covered bridges are rare to nonexistent in my erstwhile home of Alaska, yet are liberally scattered across New York State. This one extended across a ravine with sharp rocks and fast-moving water at the bottom. Trees and thick brush crowded in around the entrance and creepers festooned the wooden roof. Sketchy as hell.

Lionel said, "Maybe regroup and try it when there's not a lady present?"

"Hey!" Krystal said. "I'm in this. Ken and Roger are family. Don't think for one goddamned second you're gonna ditch me that easy."

The unpleasant truth? I didn't wish any ill upon Krystal. Neither did I feel much concern over her potential exposure to danger.

"Minerva, sit," I said. She wasn't pleased.

I walked down the hill to the bridge. Rushing water grew loud and the structure was more decrepit and lopsided the closer I came. Left hand gripping the rail, I carefully put weight on the warped boards. Metal and wood trembled as I advanced. Two-thirds of the way across, pieces of board had rotted and plunged into the creek. I skirted the hole and made it to the other side. My companions crossed without any problem. Minerva looked at me like I was a king-sized moron. She sniffed me and licked hands, worried and angry. Lionel grimaced. He and I shared a peculiar wavelength; neither of us could shake the impression that an indefinable menace lurked. The smart thing, when your sixth and seventh senses are ringing alarm bells, is to pack your marbles and go home.

But we had guns and a job to do.

The main trail curved south, then west, increasingly overgrown and crisscrossed by fallen trees. We traveled the less obvious path along a meandering deer track, and inevitably arrived at the X on the map. The derelict house sat among evergreens and a clutch of saplings and bushes. Sections of its peaked roof were stove in by shorn limbs, windows smashed and patched with decaying tarpaper. Chaos symbols were sprayed in faded yellow and red across the entry door hanging loose on its upper hinge. Broken bottles glinted in the charcoal of bonfires. One dry-rotted power pole, sheared at its apex. Faint traces of a driveway angled south, ever south. Overgrown and overcome. Meth-heads might be sleeping inside the house, or a roving band of teenage Satanists. Anything was possible. Anything, except I instantly knew the Barnhouses weren't bunkered in this shack, much less recording their masterpiece.

What if they're dangling from hooks in the cellar? The worst scenario always has a greater than zero probability. Which meant I had to gird my loins like the idiot heroes of yore and venture into the lair of the unknown.

Lionel thumbed the Mossberg's safety. Krystal stepped closer to him.

She said, "This is horrible. Please, tell me this isn't the right spot. Please don't tell me this is where we'll find them."

I couldn't disagree. Bad, bad vibes.

Spongy gnarls and disks of gray fungus repelled me and I savored neither the reeking mold, nor how the birds' raucous clamor had ceased. Pale streamers of light shined through the canopy dome. The sun, partially blotted, swung in an arc toward the distant peaks. I'd camped in far remoter sites and slept an untroubled sleep. Had done plenty of tours in urban jungles, too. I harkened to an offhand comment by program director, Judd Aker on refusing to hang around his radio station after sundown. Mom had believed there are intrinsically hostile locations—suburban homes that have seen domestic violence, fields of carnage, and virgin wilderness. Occasionally, these represented intersections of the natural and hypernatural. We were at the precipice of such a junction, a genius loci, as Roger Barnhouse mentioned. My rational mind could arm-wrestle its atavistic counterpart the whole livelong day. Neither wanted to be caught here after sundown.

A mockingbird screamed, childlike, fearful.

CHAPTER SIXTEEN
(Wails & Moans II)

"Krystal, watch our backs," I said to be polite. "Lionel and I will sweep and clear. Two, three minutes, tops."

The lady did not protest.

I drew my revolver, unleashed Minerva, and entered the doorway. She pressed against my calf. I'd paid a military specialist a small fortune to instill in her the basics of combat tactics. Money well spent. Intelligent, aggressive, and brave, a man couldn't have designed a more dependable partner for hairy situations. Her presence certainly reduced the odds of some backwoods lunatic springing an ambush.

It went smoothly. I moved left; Lionel dipped right. The murkily illuminated ground floor was a hedge maze cluttered with collapsed roofing, timbers, and detritus. Three side rooms in bad shape, but not hiding any druggies or cultists. Although, people had squatted in the dim past: trash (more bottles, soggy porno mags, and posters of various rockers), graffiti, and destroyed furniture. Details coalesced as I took stock. Rusted, water-damaged recording equipment slightly sheltered by overhanging remnants of the roof. Mixing and sound consoles, a recording booth, and such. Jackpot. This could be none other than Wails and Moans, the fabled secret studio.

I whistled.

Krystal entered the house first and moved straight to the petrified mixing console and laid her hand upon it the way a pilgrim worships at a shrine.

"Oh no. Jesus. "Where the hell are you guys?" she said to the moldy nothingness. Then, to me, "Fucking told you they weren't collaborating on fuck all."

We conducted a brisk search of the premises. Shadows lengthened. Had the brothers visited recently, there might be evidence. Fresh food wrappers, pocket lint, anything. Fruitless except for a battery-operated recorder I discovered tucked into a cabinet. I pressed play, expecting nothing, and nearly had a heart attack when a cultured voice began to orate through waves of background static:

On October 19, the year of our Lord 2017, an object, some twelve hundred meters in length, will enter the edge of our solar system from interstellar space. Astronomers monitoring its trajectory and behavior will speculate that it may be manned or directed by an alien intelligence. This incursion will represent the second within a two-year span—

THE WIND BEGAN TO HOWL

The narration slowed into garbled gibberish, then the batteries gave up the ghost.

Krystal covered her mouth.

"Ken. That's his voice…He recorded a screed predicting an international news story, the asteroid or whatever."

"When did he make this prediction?" I said.

"2012, 2013. He and Roger claimed to share a vivid dream. When it actually came to pass, they were glued to the TV for a week, manic as fuck. Ranted about how this proved the supercollider in Horseheads shouldn't have been abandoned. Burned the midnight oil writing, drawing, making freaky recordings. I mean, it was also totally in character for those geeks. Then people called. Unlisted numbers, heavy breathing, clicking on the line. Occasionally, a computer would recite serial numbers, poetry. Continued for a month. We were living at the apartment in Saugerties. Ken grabbed my arm one day and warned me not to answer the phone. He was crazed. Fucking flat affect. I moved to Kingston soon after. Couldn't deal anymore." She breathed deeply and visibly pulled herself together.

Lionel pulled aside jags of sheetrock and a filthy blanket to reveal a metal sarcophagus propped against a wall. The metal casket was balanced upright, its front panel fashioned as a leering demonic visage. A rusted lever jutted from the side. Of course, sarcophagus and casket were the wrong words.

"This what I think it is?" he said.

"Replica iron maiden." I conjured the image of a bed of nails, tiny holes to vent the blood. Odd, albeit the sort of prop one could plausibly expect of a cult rock duo or their bizzarro producer.

"A bit on the nose considering the venue." He lit a cigarette. "Man, I hate to say it. Can't be a body inside. Right...?"

"Iron maidens weren't used in torture. A dumbass myth." Krystal stroked the bas-relief visage. "Museums and rich assholes read some medieval horror story and decided to make some to scare the rubes."

"Terror flicks were bullshitting me since I was a little kid glued to Vincent Price's every move?"

"Afraid so." She laughed and dabbed her nose with a tissue.

"Horror comics lied?" Lionel licked his thumb and wiped a splotch of mascara from her cheek.

Minerva's entire body stiffened. She snarled. For a dizzying moment, my imagination ran wild and I heard tap-tapping and beheld the iron maiden creak open, a scabrous, partially bandaged hand clutching the lid, and behind that, a gangling, leprous form born of Friday night creature features—a mummy, a ghoul, a skeletal lich, revived into demonic undeath, lusting for warm flesh and shiny souls. However, Minerva wasn't glaring at the iron maiden. Rather, her gaze focused with laser beam intensity upon a gaping hole in the wall where the back door had fallen.

Cordell Harms, resembling his corporate photograph, and clad in loose-fitting hunting clothes, nodded genially. Dorian Gray with a pistol.

"Greetings, fellow travelers. Mr. Coleridge, I trust you will keep your pet under control. Else it's a bullet in the brain. Same goes for the doggy."

The mockingbird whooped. Its cry sounded like, *Help! Help!*

Which is how I realized, an instant too late, that Polanski and Cher were creeping up behind us.

The sands drained from the hourglass in a hurry. Harms and his flunkies toted automatics. Lionel and I had what we had. In a way, I counted myself fortunate. The bad guys could've been strapped with rifles and sniped us from a distance. They'd likely seen my files, same as Urban, but evidently it hadn't impressed them. Point in my favor. I eased to one side and shifted my position so I could keep everyone in sight. Gun up, not directed anywhere specific. Lionel drew a bead on Polanski and Cher. They returned the sentiment.

"Lying sack of shit," Krystal said. "Where's Ken?"

"Be quiet," Harms said.

"How long have worked for Svengali?" I said to Krystal. "Since the boys saw you hitching that fateful night? I bet you were a plant from the jump."

"You're sharper than you look. What tipped my hand?"

"Nothing, everything. I'm on guard against femme fatales. You aren't a good liar. Guess you're not a pro." I didn't mention the fact Roger Barnhouse had warned me in his cryptic manner. No need to twist the knife.

"Flash some thigh and you've already won. No spy skillset required. Sandy said it best—*anybody* can be an asset."

"The Barnhouses are a pair of gullible sonsofbitches. Real patsies."

Mild as ever, Harms said, "Krys, I won't tell you again."

She ignored him.

"It started that way. My job was to leash them, persuade them to Cordell's way of thinking. Somewhere along the line, I had a change of heart. Convinced them they were being duped, led to slaughter. He's plotted to remove me from the picture since they fired his ass after *The Colossal Nothing*. Sent his minions to kill me at the apartment. Probably triggered by your involvement."

"Actually, I had a completely different plan." Harms pointed the gun at her, which suited me fine. "I regret my forbearance, believe you me."

"Cordell, shut up," I said. And to Krystal, "You arranged this meeting."

She said, "Man, I had no idea where the studio was. However, yeah…I texted him this morning and said *my* thugs were closing in. Hoped to flush him

THE WIND BEGAN TO HOWL

into the open. Here he is. Figured you and blondie could handle it. Can you?"

"Hi, boys." Sandahl Urban stepped around a partial wall behind Cher and Polanski. She carried a can of bear mace in each fist.

Krystal snapped her fingers.

"Oh, yeah. I called her, too."

"Wish you would've called the cops instead," Lionel said through his teeth.

I chuckled at the lunacy of the situation. Especially hilarious to glimpse Gil and Fischer sneaking around the front door three seconds prior to the commencement of the Peckinpah bloodbath.

"We came in the opposite way," Urban said. "Much faster. Cordell, there are people in Langley who will be eager to interview you about whatever black ops program you're involved with. I'm gonna get my gold star at last."

Harms nodded and it was plain he hadn't calculated these variables into his masterplan. Easy to tell he'd decided to push the self-destruct button. Such was the default behavior of such men. Then this vaguely Robert Palmer-looking motherfucker had the audacity to say:

"Bang a gong, bitches."

Clouds eclipsed the sun and the gloom thickened. I tasted sulfur and metal. The hairs on my neck prickled. Time slowed. Urban blasted her mace. I put two rounds into Harms, center mass. His pistol sparked as he pitched face-first. He raised his arm and Minerva clamped it in her jaws, whipsawing him like a rag doll. Everybody who had a piece started shooting. But it was chaos because a fog of mace hung in the air. That shit is the worst—blinds you, burns your nose and throat, so you're crying, gagging and trying to claw your eyeballs. I avoided the brunt and it still destroyed my ability to function properly. The Mossberg banged—

—I staggered into the woods, Minerva on my hip. Pure instinct to get clear of an enclosed space, to seek distance and cover. Lionel was there, bent and vomiting as he loped. He paused to splash bottled water on his face, and ran again. Gunfire popped and a bullet zipped past my ear and tore bark off a tree. We separated, putting a few yards between us. To my left lay a deep, deep ravine full of smokey shadows; servants' entrance to Hades. The forest lay in twilight; a woodcut realm of fairies and goblins, of wolves with glowing eyes and clabbered jaws. The gods of the underworld leaned on the edges of their seats. We stumbled from tree to tree exchanging gunfire with bogies running parallel and slightly behind. Swimming in darkness, revolver extended—bullets vectored like slow orange tracers. I didn't discern any figures, only muzzle flashes. Sound traveled strangely, bouncing and muffled. Up was down, the needle on a compass spun, no goddamned notion which direction we fled—perhaps in a circle of blood. What had I said

THE WIND BEGAN TO HOWL

about this trip? Bugs in a jar. Yes, indeed, we were in a killing jar. This wasn't material reality, but an astral nightmare realm.

—Slumped against a pine trunk to reload, I witnessed Lionel and Cher fronting like gunfighters at ten paces. They opened up simultaneously—he with the booming canon of a shotgun, she with a teeny-tiny automatic. She popped off three or four rounds before the Mossberg blast cut her mostly in half—

—Polanski, features bloated, frothing at the mouth, materialized from the underbrush almost on top of me, which surprised both of us. I recovered first. *Blam!* times six. He crouched and fired at me twice. First bullet hit dead center and set me on my ass. Thank you, body armor. Don't know where the second bullet went, but he must've been out too because he flung his piece at me and rushed straight in. I rolled to my knees and he tried to catch my neck in some sort of hold. A mistake; he was better off picking me apart with jabs and kicks, but the forest floor wasn't stable like Krystal Niven's apartment. Dirt and leaves slid underfoot and when the earth shifts; instinct will encourage combatants to clinch, to cling. I backhanded him with the revolver, which I expected to take his head off, or stun him, at least. Polanski didn't appreciate it. Loosened his teeth for sure. Didn't stop him, though. He grasped my right wrist with his left hand and rammed the fingers of his right hand at my eyeballs. Holy fucking ow, better to kill me than hurt me. Our previous encounter taught me a lesson or two. I twisted my head away and surged to my feet, calling down the hideous red light. I radiated the heat of a red star. Primeval, atavistic power coursed through my veins. Strength of the Neanderthal, the sabertooth tiger. Once I seized his body, it was all over for him.

I love the Olympic standby, the hammer throw. So much adrenaline cooked in my veins I could've knocked an elephant down. Instead, I grasped that bony shit by his collar and belt, lifted his next-to-nothing body, whirled us in a full circle, driving with my hips as I extended my arms, and let go. A surreal moment. Felt like God hooked Billy and snatched him. He arced, flailing, and disappeared into the ravine. Brush crackled down in the gulf, the way it does when a heavy object crashes through it.

The red light snuffed and I bent double, depleted. Sobbing and gasping, half-scabbed psychic wounds opened in a cascade of minor torments.

"Why is this so goddamned hard?" The gods declined to answer.

Lionel threw back his head and laughed defiantly. He didn't appear to have any bullet holes in him.

"Well, that was pretty cool." He popped the tab on a can of beer. It was smashed and leaking. He guzzled the remainder, licked foam from his hands, and wiped his mouth with his sleeve. "I think we killed all of them."

THE WIND BEGAN TO HOWL

We circled back to the studio. Urban and Gil tended to Krystal. She'd been hit in the shoulder and leg. Conscious, pale, trembling with shock. Fischer had removed his shirt and wrapped it around his hand. Gil informed me they'd summoned the police. Whether the gendarmes would arrive in minutes or hours was an open question.

"Jesus Hopfrog Christ," Gil said. "I wouldn't have agreed to come back if I'd known it was the fucking OK Corral."

"Where is Harms?" Lionel poked the shotgun barrel at a patch of raw, scuffed earth in the shape of a body.

Nobody knew.

I told them to hold down the fort until the cops made the scene. Lionel and I trotted a short distance and picked up Harms' blood trail.

CHAPTER SEVENTEEN
(Shout at the Devil)

Half a mile on, a granite and shale cliff reared some forty feet like Mother Nature's own roadblock. Minerva led our pack. She plowed east along the base of the rise, snout in the dirt. Harms was a quart or two low by now. His blood spattered the bushes.

Another two hundred yards, I spied the entrance to the bunker. Someone had taken pains to conceal the entrance with camouflage tarps and a humongous screen of brush. If I hadn't been on the alert, I might've passed by, none the wiser. Also, Harms lay on the ground, dead as the dirt. Closer inspection revealed fresh tire tracks in the leaves near his corpse. A four-wheeler and trailer was my best estimate. Jogging in armor isn't a joy. We rested at the entrance of the bunker for a minute. A good excuse to recover my breath. Who knew whether there were any more bogies. I wasn't eager to get shot while blundering into the fortification. We listened for any signs of activity within. Silence, except for the forest noises.

Here was the moment of crisis—finish the mission or quit. I had a strong hunch we'd never know the truth if we didn't see it through. This was the sort of mess people in high places swept under carpets. Lionel gauged my expression. He took point to sweep for tripwires and pressure plates.

The steel doors were sprung, corroded with neglect, and permanently wedged by rocks and sloughed soil. He pushed aside the tarp and shined his cellphone beam into a dank opening. Pretty quick, all three of us entered and traversed a short tunnel with two sharp bends that let into a long, narrow chamber. There we gathered upon a filthy concrete floor. The concrete walls sloped to the ceiling. Floor and walls were cracked. Water dripped steadily and the place smelled green as the belly of a swamp and fetid with the rot and shit of nesting animals. No obvious power supply, yet I saw a switch and flipped it. Fluorescent track lights emitted a cruel, ghastly radiance like Virgil clapping on the lamps in a circle of hell. I took in the décor—several lockers and tool chests; a metal worktable cluttered with circuit boards, coils of tubing and wires, transistors, and assorted small tools. Crates draped in more tarps, a small diesel generator, and a rank of industrial batteries that you'd typically find inside heavy equipment. At the rear, a cargo elevator cage.

"Would hate to be trapped here when the three bears come home." Lionel tapped his phone. "No reception." He noticed me eyeing the hatch. "Keypad lock. Unless you're Kreskin…"

Yes, a keypad locked the wheel of the elevator. No, I'm not Kreskin. However, I'd pretended to be a detective long enough to start thinking like one. I tried several combos. Astronomers discovered the Boötes Void in 1981. Entered in reverse, 1891, did the trick like open sesame.

"See any surveillance cameras?" he said. "I sure don't."

"Harms was off the books, running a shoestring op. Probably not a commando team in there. I'll take my chances." I patted Minerva and instructed her to stay. It would've been nice to breach the unknown lair as a trio, but the risk of getting trapped was too awful a fate to risk.

There were two buttons on the panel. I hit the down arrow.

The cage descended into a murky shadowland. There dwelt Pluto, Whiro, Lucifer, and the dread hosts and retinues of such inglorious presences. It dropped from the ceiling of a cavern.

My phone went blue screen and remained inert. Possibly why there weren't any cameras installed. Strings of chemical bulbs illuminated a small portion of what I suspected to be an immense gallery. The rock walls were studded with clusters of milky white crystals ranging in size from a fist to nodes that could've crushed a bus if they'd fallen onto one. Humid breezes moaned in crevices and chimneys and ruffled my hair. Fast moving water roared somewhere in the deep. Stranger noises rode astride the thunder; elemental screams and flickers of magma-hot light. I'm not ashamed to admit the nature of these sounds frightened me, tempted me to tuck tail and retreat to the surface, let the authorities do whatever they wished.

Two hundred feet down, give or take. At the bottom, I walked through a garden of crystals along a broad shelf hanging over an abyss. Busy beavers had erected three modular sheds, very much on par with utility structures on construction sites. Two equipment sheds with cattle doors and an office-residential module. Ceramic turbines were embedded at intervals, connected by cables snaking along the ground and into an enormous gyroscope mounted atop a platform. Inside the gyroscope was Kenneth Barnhouse, naked and spread eagle as the Vitruvian Man. A technician in funky retro-space-age earphones and filthy coveralls fiddled with instruments on a console. The gyroscope rotated, sluggish and wobbly, smoothing as it gained momentum. I was too close for my health, but not close enough to stop what happened next.

Ken Barnhouse wore a mask over his jaw, styled in a similar bizarre fashion as the engineer's earphones.

THE WIND BEGAN TO HOWL

The prisoner moaned; it issued with an electronic distortion. Nearer crystals responded with flickers, then fully illuminated, pulsing in pinks and violets. He thrashed against his bonds and howled. Concentric rings of slashing reds and violets rippled outward, rushed over a curtain of flowstone, and bored a technicolor hole. It very easily might've drilled to the center of the earth. His unearthly shriek was trailed by lesser echoes of his voice. Tesla jags of electricity jumped between the crystal nodes and tuning forks surmounting the turbines. My knees buckled with the hammer-smash of sonic agony. Zapped me with the afterimage of boiling suns spinning like the dial slots on a rotary phone. I covered my head with my arms.

The gyroscope spun down. Ken Barnhouse sagged, limp and spent. Simultaneously, the plasma lightshow reversed itself. The borehole sealed and the crystals darkened, ring by ring, sucking in the heat and the last few whispers of sound. I rose on unsteady legs and approached the engineer as he jotted notes on a clipboard. The bastard was reaching for the switch to juice his subject for another ride when I smacked the back of his skull with my revolver.

CHAPTER EIGHTEEN
(Pacts)

As I'd suspected, somebody in authority slammed closed the book on the incident. Yes, statements were taken, papers filed. Plainclothes gentlemen administered the third degree to me in a little room in Albany. Justified shootings and sundry beatings. We'd put the kibosh on an unspecified, albeit sinister, criminal operation. The higher-ups couldn't bestow medals and were reluctant to air dirty laundry in open court, so they split the difference. Go forth and sin no more was essentially the injunction. Sandahl Urban gave me a conspiratorial wink the last time we crossed paths after the initial debriefing.

Rumors abounded. Ken Barnhouse survived, although he became a permanent resident at an Upstate institute, complete with an armed guard and a battery of stoic G-men in black suits and shades. Harms' people had somehow integrated the mask-amplifier to Ken's nervous system. Krystal spent some quality time at a hospital before disappearing into the woodwork. Gil's film sank into development hell. Last I heard, Fischer and Urban were happily globetrotting, none the worse for the wear. Who financed Cordell Harms? What in God's name were they doing? I filed those under unsolved mysteries.

One detail haunts me—after I detached Ken Barnhouse from his harness, I lugged him topside and made him as comfortable as I could. We were alone for a long while, waiting for Lionel to guide the rescue team and the cops to the bunker. I'd briefly searched for Roger without discovering any traces.

"He escaped," Ken Barnhouse said. He could barely speak through the amplifier, which elicited convulsions when I tried to pry it loose. The mouth aperture carried his voice and rendered it comprehensible. "Got loose. Got loose."

Presently I was able to piece together his meaning. Roger had somehow broken out of the prison shack. He shouted a hole—a portal according to Ken—into solid rock and hurled himself in as it shut.

"He's alive," Ken said, choking and slobbering as his agitation spiked. "He's singing down there. He's singing. Listen."

An investigator placidly relayed the engineer had testified that Roger Barnhouse leaped to his death in the crevasse below the laboratory. Ken was obviously stark raving mad.

I couldn't shake the momentary clarity in Ken Barnhouse's gaze.

"He's singing. Listen. Listen."

The first night home, I felt shattered, yet numb. Meg fixed dinner and didn't push as I sat, smiling and not eating or talking much. She held my hand on the couch during a movie. A Kurosawa epic; one of my favorites. I drank far too much and vaguely recall staggering to bed, dim shrieks of samurai in my ears.

Around midnight, I crawled out of the covers, went into Devlin's room and lay on the floor, weeping. Minerva climbed on top of my aching chest and clung. I clung right back.

"I can't do this anymore." Was it a vow or a plea? Was it even me talking to the ghosts, the angels, dread undertaker Whiro grinning between cracks in the earth?

Come dawn, I was myself again, more or less.

One night in the lonesome October, Devlin requested Lionel and I indulge him on a backyard expedition. We trekked into the boonies behind the house, hung a lantern, pitched tents, and roasted marshmallows over a cheery campfire. Lionel told a couple of ghost stories he claimed were true. Devlin declared them pretty good. He swore to stay up all night, then promptly conked out. I tucked him in and cracked a bottle of whiskey.

Lionel smoked a cigarette and scratched Minerva's ears.

"The eve of the dead approacheth."

I sighed.

"God help me. What's on your mind?"

"Ever see anything when you hovered at death's door?"

"Such as the Pearly Gates? Valkyries on pegasi?"

"Yeah."

"Which time, brother?"

He smiled, crooked and bitter.

"And you?" I said. "What did you see on the other side? God send you back?"

Lionel's expression froze.

"No near deaths on my ledger. Blackouts and getting knocked for a loop, yes."

"Share with the class. You kicked this off." I passed the bottle.

"Remember the cover of *Wish You Were Here*? The dude on fire shaking hands with the other dude? Like that, except it was you and me and both of us were burning." He swigged. "I'm chapped we couldn't get Barnhouse to sign that waiver, or forge his sig, or I dunno. Our bonus shot in the ass. Those lawyers ever complain?"

THE WIND BEGAN TO HOWL

"Nary a word. Although, since you've broached the subject and we've crossed into the witching hour…" I reached into my coat.

"C'mon. You have it on you? Why?"

"My theory is, Urban was right. The Barnhouses *were* cursed. Remember disappearing ink? We were obsessed with it as kids."

"Scribble a message in lemon juice. Invisible. Apply heat and voila! Words appear. Second grade David Copperfield, baby."

I set the lantern on a rock and examined the envelope containing the Barnhouse contract. Originally pristine white, the envelope had gradually stained as if dunked in wine. Script in the corner read: *Clupach, Ransom, & Friend*. My shadow danced on the bole of a pine tree. Midnight in an Edwardian cemetery, except this was midnight in the deep woods in the Rondout Valley, 21st Century USA.

I extracted the contract sheaf. Its properties had also dramatically altered since I unsealed the envelope in the presence of Red McLaren several weeks prior. Parchment crackled when unfolded. Smelled rich and musty as if it had nestled on an antiquarian's shelf for a century or two. Neatly handwritten with curlicues and flourishes. I read it twice, imagining a quill scratching by kerosene lamplight. I handed it to Lionel.

"Okay. Freaky." He tossed the papers into my lap with the vigor of a man snake bitten. He dragged and exhaled. "Immutable is not a word you see every day."

We stared into the firepit coals. Neither of us wasted a breath on the obvious stuff—such as the fact the "agreement" was obviously a hoax; even if sincere, no court would uphold a medieval compact that if executed, by its very nature, violated any number of laws and customs, secular and otherwise. A stiff breeze rustled the canopy. Branches groaned a collective warning; we'd rushed headlong well past summer's end.

Lionel cupped his hands to light another cigarette. Before he put the Zippo away, I extended the contract. He snicked his lighter and held the flame to the corner of the parchment. Stubborn, it finally curled and blackened. All at once it disintegrated in a red flash of smoke like a magician's trick.

"Abracadabra," I said. The wind kicked up.

ACKNOWLEDGMENTS

While drafting this novella, I fell deathly ill. Not long after its completion, I collapsed and was rushed to surgery for a respiratory infection. I spent five weeks recovering in the hospital. That recovery is ongoing. The fact I'm here to write these acknowledgements is due to the care I received from the staff at Westchester and Mid-Hudson Regional hospitals. My deepest gratitude to everyone who worked to save my life and rehabilitate me so I could return home to Jessica M and our faithful hound, Valentina.

Thank you to the community of family, friends, colleagues, and readers who donated time, money, and emotional support. I'm still opening cards and letters from all over the globe. The outpouring sustained me during some dark hours and fills me with joy at the prospect of a second chance—the opportunity to unravel more of Coleridge's saga in the years ahead.

Special thanks to Mike Davis; John, Fiona, and

David Langan; Paul Tremblay; Ed Maciag; Norm "I Didn't Hear No Bell" Partridge; Chris McLaren; Greg Greene; Yves Tourigny; Priya Sharma; Kris Dikeman; Timbi Barron; Sean Cosby; Kelly Link; Jeff Ford; Scott Lynch; Gordon White; Elizabeth Hand; Livia Llewellyn; Ellen Datlow; Jordan Hamessley, Pouya Shahbazian, and the entire team at New Leaf Literary; and my beloved Jessica M.

Thank you to Mayra Fersner for the knockout cover art. Finally, I'm indebted to Doug Murano for his faith and generosity.

LAIRD BARRON was born in Alaska, where he raised huskies and worked in the construction and fishing industries for much of his youth. He is the author of several short story collections and five novels, and his work has also appeared in many magazines and anthologies. A multiple Locus, World Fantasy, and Bram Stoker award nominee, he is also a three-time winner of the Shirley Jackson Award. Barron lives in Kingston, NY.

Printed in the United States
by Baker & Taylor Publisher Services